THE

RED
UMBRELLA

Christina Diaz Gonzalez

Alfred A. Knopf

New York

THIS IS A BORZOI BOOK PUBLISHED BY ALFRED A. KNOPF

Visit us on the Web! www.randomhouse.com/kids

Educators and librarians, for a variety of teaching tools, visit us at
www.randomhouse.com/teachers

Library of Congress Cataloging-in-Publication Data
Gonzalez, Christina Diaz.
The red umbrella / Christina Diaz Gonzalez. — 1st ed.
    p. cm.
Summary: In 1961 after Castro has come to power in Cuba, fourteen-year-old Lucia and her seven-year-old brother are sent to the United States when her parents, who are not in favor of the new regime, fear that the children will be taken away from them as others have been.
ISBN 978-0-375-86190-1 (trade) — ISBN 978-0-375-96190-8 (lib. bdg.) —
ISBN 978-0-375-89628-6 (e-book)
1. Cuba—History—1959–1990—Juvenile fiction. [1. Cuba—History—1959–1990—Fiction. 2. Family life—Cuba—Fiction.] I. Title.
PZ7.G5882Re 2010
[Fic]—dc22
2009022309

The text of this book is set in 13-point Cochin.

Printed in the United States of America
May 2010
10 9 8 7 6 5 4 3 2 1

First Edition

For my sons, Peter and Daniel

Chapter 1

CASTRO RULES OUT ELECTIONS IN CUBA
—*THE NEW YORK TIMES*, MAY 2, 1961

I watched as a white heron circled the beach and then headed north toward the open waters of the tropics. The lone bird flapped its wings, gradually disappearing into the pink-and-orange-streaked sky. It was time for us to go, too.

"Pack it up, Frankie. It's getting late," I said.

Frankie threw his small fishing net into the rolling surf. "C'mon, Lucía . . . a few more minutes. We don't even have school tomorrow."

I sighed and leaned back on my towel. Frankie was right, there was no need to rush home. Since all the private schools had been closed and the public schools were being reevaluated, who knew when classes would start again. I was growing tired of constantly hearing about the revolution, but I privately thanked Castro for postponing my algebra test. I closed my eyes and imagined old Señora Cardoza, our eighth-grade teacher, being questioned by one of the new government officials. The poor woman would probably be so flustered that she'd pass out. Then I thought of Manuel, who sat two rows ahead of me in algebra class. With his light brown hair and green eyes, he was definitely the cutest boy in class. Maybe that's why I couldn't concentrate on anything Señora Cardoza said.

A distant rumbling snapped me out of my daydream. I searched the sky to see if a storm was coming, but it was a clear evening. The thunder-like noise grew. Something big was coming down the beachside road. I shook the sand off my feet, grabbed my sandals, and hurried toward the boardwalk. A caravan of large camouflaged trucks and jeeps came into view. I half hid behind a coconut palm and watched as truck after truck, filled with men wearing fatigues, roared past me. During the past year, there had been pictures of the revolution's soldiers in the newspapers and on TV, but I'd never seen so many in person. Most of the soldiers that were riding in the trucks looked like they were in their twenties, but a few seemed to be my age. One of them had such intensity and fierce determination in his eyes that it made me shudder, and I quickly looked away.

And then they were gone, leaving behind a cloud of sand and dust in the road.

"Did you see that?" Frankie yelled from the water's edge.

I turned and walked back to where my bike and beach towel lay. "Yeah. Strange to see army trucks around here."

"Huh? I'm talking about the huge yellowtail that swam . . ." Frankie pulled in his net and spun around. "Wait, those were army trucks?"

"Yeah, but they're already gone." I shook out my towel and carefully tucked it into the bike's front-hanging basket. "*Vámonos*, Frankie, we're going to be late for dinner."

"You sure they're gone?" Frankie looked toward the road.

"I'm sure. Nothing ever happens in Puerto Mijares. Those soldiers were probably just driving through."

"Well, you can go home. I'll catch up later." He stared at the waist-deep water surrounding him.

"Ha! Mamá would have my head if I left you alone."

"I'm already seven. I don't need a babysitter." He twisted his body, getting ready to throw the net again.

Frankie could be stubborn, but I knew the one thing my little brother loved more than fishing. "Okay, I guess we'll both have to miss Mamá's *flan*."

"*¿Flan?*" Frankie pulled at the net, already in mid-air, catching it with his left hand. "Why didn't you say that before?" He sprinted out of the water and hurried over to his bike. A sly smile crept onto his face. "Hey, Lucy," he said, and with one swift move, he snatched my towel and threw it as far as he could. "Race you home!"

❈　❈　❈　❈　❈

My bike screeched into the driveway. I jumped off, hurdled the potted plant sitting by the porch steps, and ran to the front door. "Beat you again," I laughed, stumbling into the house.

An eerie silence greeted me.

"Mamá? Papá?" I called out. There was an uneasiness hanging in the air as I walked into the darkened family room.

Frankie clattered into the house. "You only won because I let you."

"Shhh. Something's wrong," I whispered.

"*¿Qué?*"

"Not sure." I headed toward the dimly lit kitchen.

My parents were sitting at the kitchen table huddled around a radio, oblivious to the fact that the sun had set and that most of the house was now dark and full of shadows.

"Oh, *hijos*, you're home." Mamá immediately stood up, smoothed back her dark hair, and gave us quick kisses on the cheek. She signaled for Papá to turn down the radio. The voice of someone giving a speech was promptly silenced.

"What's going on? Why is the house so dark?" I asked.

Mamá turned on some lights and took out the dinner plates.

"Nothing's happened." Papá smiled, but the worried look in his eyes betrayed him. "Your mother and I just lost track of time listening to the radio. Did you have fun at the beach?"

"It was okay, but I didn't catch anything. I did see this huge yellowtail . . . about this big!" Frankie opened his arms wide.

Papá chuckled. "That big, huh? Probably more like this." He brought Frankie's arms together until they were about a foot apart.

"Well, yeah, maybe." Frankie reached for the plate of sliced avocado.

"Mamá, do you need help with dinner?" I asked, peering over her shoulder to see what she was cooking.

"No, it's just leftovers from yesterday." She turned as Frankie went for his second slice. "Frankie, *no comas más*. You'll get filled up before dinner. Now wash up . . . both of you. Dinner will be ready in five minutes."

"You made *flan*, right?" Frankie wiped his sticky hands on his shorts.

"Oh, the *flan*. I forgot, with everything—"

"Ahem." Papá cleared his throat.

"I'll make it tomorrow, sweetie. Promise. Now go."

"Told you we shouldn't have left the beach," Frankie muttered as we stepped into the hallway.

I ignored him and focused instead on the shouting coming from the kitchen radio. Mamá had raised the volume the moment we'd left the room. A reporter was describing a large crowd gathered near the town square, and in the background there was some sort of chanting. I strained to hear what they were saying. Then the words came through clearly, echoing in my head. *¡Socialismo o muerte!* Socialism . . . or death!

Chapter 2

U.S. Brands Cuba Communist State,
Says Castro Outdoes Soviet in Barring Vote,
Likens His Rallies to Hitler's
—*The New York Times*, May 3, 1961

"Today I'm having real fun," I mumbled to myself.

I pulled open the bedroom drapes and took a look outside. The brightness of the morning sun blinded me for a moment. Then, as my eyes adjusted to the light, I realized what a perfect day it was. The cloudless sky, the slight chatter of birds in the fruit trees, and the warm breeze that brushed past my cheek . . . there was no place I'd rather be, although Ivette and I did talk about visiting Paris or Rome someday. We'd been best friends since kindergarten, and I couldn't imagine exploring those cities without her. But for now, we'd have to be happy spending the day walking around downtown Puerto Mijares. We could catch a movie or even a double feature. Something by Fellini was probably playing.

I thumbed through my closet and picked out a pleated emerald-green skirt with a crisply ironed white shirt. It wasn't too fancy or too casual. After all, you never knew who we might run into in town. But choosing a headband was a bit harder. I loved my bright yellow one, which would stand out against my dark hair, but the green and white polka-dot one matched my outfit perfectly. This was a decision better left for Ivette. She was my fashion guru.

A thumping on the stairs let me know that Frankie was on his way to the kitchen. The warm, sweet smell of *café con leche* had wafted its way up to me, and my stomach growled in response. Breakfast was probably already on the table.

I wondered if everything was back to normal after the strangeness of the night before. The house had felt so quiet, and it was odd for both Mamá and Papá to choose to hear news reports on the radio instead of watching TV with us. But the bright sun chased away those shadows. Why worry when the day held so many possibilities? I grabbed my pink robe and headed downstairs before Frankie could devour everything Mamá had made.

"Mamá, today I'm catching the biggest fish in the ocean. I can feel it," Frankie said, stuffing a freshly fried *croqueta* in his mouth.

"*Buenos días.*" I walked into the kitchen to find Mamá slicing a loaf of bread.

"Oh, Lucía, you're up. Good, I was waiting for you to come downstairs. I need to talk to the two of you."

I stopped in my tracks. Babysitting Frankie the day before was one thing, but spending the entire school break with a seven-year-old was completely unfair. This unexpected vacation was supposed to be enjoyed with my friends. I looked for Papá, who usually agreed with me. There were only two plates on the table, and the white serving platter in the middle held only six small, ham-filled *croquetas*, barely enough for Frankie and me.

"Where's Papá?" I asked.

"He had to go to work early." Mamá put down the knife and walked over to the table. "I have a favor to ask the both of you. It's about—"

"So he already left?"

"Yes, they called him from the bank early this morning." Mamá pointed to the chair next to Frankie. "*Mi hija, siéntate.*"

A wave of disappointment came over me. I was going to get stuck with Frankie again. He'd tag along all day as Ivette and I walked around downtown. I sank into the seat next to my brother.

"*Niños,* it's about the revolution. You know things in Cuba have changed, especially in the last few months."

Air. I felt like I could breathe again. This was a talk

about the revolution and not about more babysitting. I smiled at my mother. "Mamá, we know. We hear about it in school *all* the time." I took the same nasal, monotone voice of my revolution-loving social-studies teacher. "Comandante Fidel is making our lives better. He has replaced corruption with a new system of government that has brought much happiness to all the Cuban people. We are living in a great time. Everything will be fair and equal for all citizens."

"Well, it's not really about being fair. That's why I wanted to—"

"It *is* fair. Señor Pedraza, our new principal, showed us." Frankie reached for some orange juice.

"*Eh?* What do you mean he *showed* you?" Mamá raised one of her perfectly drawn eyebrows.

"Señor Pedraza showed us with a secret experiment." Frankie took a big sip of juice. "Last week, before the school closed, he had us all pray that everyone would have ice cream when they got home. He told us to pray really hard . . . and I did, because you know how much I love ice cream."

"Mmm-hmm," Mamá answered as Frankie grabbed another *croqueta*.

"So, everybody prayed, but the next day, only a couple of kids said they had any. Señor Pedraza said that didn't seem very fair."

I laughed. "Yeah, but that's because—"

"I'm not done with my story!" Frankie glared.

"*Sigue,* tell me what happened next." Mamá spun her wedding ring around her finger. The diamond disappeared and then reappeared with each turn.

Frankie took a deep breath and turned back to Mamá. "Well, Señor Pedraza told us to close our eyes again and this time to ask Comandante Fidel for ice cream. A few minutes later, a lady brought enough for the whole class. Señor Pedraza said that El Comandante wouldn't leave anyone out. If one kid was going to get ice cream, then it was only right that we all got some. Now, I think *that* was super fair." Frankie licked the *croqueta* crumbs off his fingers.

Mamá shook her head. "It's not so simple."

"Yeah, goofball. God doesn't give you everything you ask for . . . if He did, I'd be allowed to wear makeup." I gave Mamá a playful look.

"All I know is that we got to eat ice cream, and that never happened when Padre Martín was in charge."

"But you understand that Fidel isn't better than God, right, Frankie?" Mamá asked.

Frankie slowly nodded.

Mamá stopped playing with her ring and rubbed her hands together. "I thought this whole Fidel thing would've been over by now. That everything would return to normal in time, but . . ."

I poured myself some *café con leche.* "Don't worry, Mamá. Nothing really changes around here."

Mamá bit her lip and shook her head. "No, Lucía,

"Lucía?"

It was pointless to argue.

"Fine," I muttered.

❖   ❖   ❖   ❖   ❖

My fun-filled day dragged slowly by as the morning blended into the afternoon. I had called Ivette right after breakfast and pretended to be sick. I didn't want to admit that I was being held hostage by my irrational mother.

"Listen," Frankie called out from the window seat, where he'd been reading a comic book. "Did you hear that?"

I walked over to him. Something was causing the window to rattle.

"It's them, isn't it?" he asked. "The soldiers."

"I don't know."

Frankie glanced around. He pointed toward the back door.

I paused to consider it, but then shook my head. "Mamá doesn't want us outside. We might get caught."

"C'mon, it's just the yard. We'll just go, take a look, and then sneak back in. Mamá is upstairs cleaning our rooms. She'll never know." Frankie tossed aside the comic book and stood up.

I grabbed him by the arm. "We promised."

"I had my fingers crossed."

"We don't know what's out there."

"Exactly!" Frankie twisted around and broke free of my grasp.

"Francisco Simón Álvarez, get back over here!" I said in my loudest whisper. "Or I'll tell Mamá."

"Fine, be a tattletale. But I'm still going, and it'll be your fault if something happens because you let me go by myself." Frankie dashed out the back door.

I had to make a decision. Keep my promise or follow Frankie. What if there *was* some sort of danger and Frankie got hurt because he was alone? I stopped thinking and darted out the door.

Chapter 3

Non-Cuban Priests to Be Expelled, Says Castro
—*The Miami Herald*, May 3, 1961

"I think the noise is coming from over there." Frankie pointed toward the high school up the street before sprinting past the front of the house.

I glanced around the neighborhood. It was strange that barely anyone was outside. "He's going to get us into so much trouble," I said to myself as I ran low to the ground so that Mamá wouldn't see me.

Soon I caught up to Frankie. He already had his eye pressed against a hole in the school's tall wooden fence.

"Okay, let's go." I tapped him on the shoulder. "Mamá is going to kill us if we get caught."

He flicked my hand away. "Whoa, wait till you see this!"

"What?"

"You're not gonna believe it."

"Let me see." I pushed him out of the way.

Peering through the hole, I could see several bearded men wearing fatigues. They were unloading boxes from army trucks while others, with rifles slung over their shoulders, walked around belting out orders. They seemed to be setting up some sort of camp behind the high school. Never had I seen so many soldiers. There seemed to be a hundred . . . or more.

From the middle of the school's baseball field, a deep voice cut through the surrounding noise. A hush fell over the soldiers as everyone stopped to stare at the small group of men that had gathered near the pitcher's mound.

"*Gusanos*, worms," yelled one of the soldiers, "tell us what we want to know!"

They were shouting at two men in business suits who were holding something behind their backs.

From where I stood, I could only see one man's profile, but he looked a lot like Papá's boss at the bank, Señor Betafil. It can't be him, I thought. He's such a sweet old man. Always giving us candy whenever we go to see Papá. What would they want with him?

"*¡Comunista!*" The old man spat out the word.

Another soldier came up from behind and struck him with a rifle butt.

"Oh!" I gasped, and turned away as the old man fell to his knees. I slowly peered through the hole again. Then I realized that the old man wasn't hiding something behind his back. His hands had been tied!

"Tell us!" The soldier pushed the other man onto the ground and placed a foot on his neck while aiming his rifle at the man's head.

I couldn't take any more. I looked away from the fence, but Frankie continued to stare at the scene through an opening at the bottom.

"Frankie, we need to go back." Mamá had been right . . . this was bad. Real bad.

"Shhh." Frankie crawled toward the corner of the fence. "I just want to see if that's—"

The sound of gunfire splintered the air. Frankie froze. Our eyes met. Neither of us made a move to see what had just happened, and a forced silence fell over the area. Not even the birds made a sound. For what seemed to be a lifetime, but was really a split second, I could only hear the soft sound of the breeze blowing through the palm trees.

Then the intensity of the soldiers' shouting and laughing swallowed me. I grabbed Frankie by his shirt collar. "Let's go. Now!"

* * * * *

Mamá peeked around my bedroom door. "*¿Todo bien, mi hija?* You've been so quiet all afternoon. I wanted to make sure you were all right."

I put down my copy of French *Vogue*. "Everything's fine." I gave her a half-smile.

Before sneaking back into the house, Frankie and I

had agreed not to say anything about the soldiers. If Mamá found out, we'd be punished for a month. Plus, for all we knew, the soldiers were just trying to scare Señor Betafil and no one really got hurt. Or maybe it wasn't even Señor Betafil. And if it was him, maybe it was the other guy who got shot because he'd done something really bad. I'd heard stories on TV of traitors being executed, but those people were trying to harm us. Could that other man have been a traitor? He must have been. The revolution wouldn't execute innocent men.

Mamá sat on my bed and started brushing my hair. "I know staying home is hard, but you and your brother have been very good." She reached over and put the silver-handled brush back on my vanity.

I bit my lip and looked down.

"You're growing up right before my eyes. In a few months, you'll have your *quinces* and a year after that I'll be chaperoning you on dates." Mamá gave me a little squeeze. "Seems like only yesterday your grandmother, God rest her soul, was chaperoning your father and me."

I looked out the window. I hated keeping secrets, but what choice did I have?

"*Escucha.* I think I hear your father." Mamá patted my hand. "Why don't you get your brother and wash up for dinner? I made my special *flan* for dessert. Today I didn't forget."

"Sure." I got up and walked across the hall to Frankie's room. From the doorway, I watched as he lined up several toy soldiers along the windowsill. He had other groups of green army men scattered on the floor.

"Dinner's almost ready," I announced.

"Uh-huh," he mumbled, focused on balancing a soldier on top of a lamp shade.

I took a step into his room. "Remember what we talked about. Don't say a word, no matter how bad you feel."

Frankie ignored me and kept playing with his toys.

"You know what I'm talking about." I knelt down next to him and lowered my voice. "What we saw . . . what the soldiers did. I think they were just trying to scare those men, but still . . ."

He paused to look at me and then turned back to his make-believe battlefield. "I don't want to talk about that."

"*Hijos*, where's your mother?" Papá stood in the doorway wearing his banker's uniform . . . dark suit, white shirt, and blue tie.

I jumped up to give him a hug, clinging to him a bit longer than usual, thankful to have him home.

Papá bent down to give me a kiss on the forehead.

I took a deep breath. I loved the way he smelled after coming home from work. A mix of cologne and the cigar he always smoked on the drive home.

"I think Mamá's in the kitchen," I answered.

"*Y tú,* Frankie?" Papá held his arms open. "You getting too big to welcome me home?"

Frankie shrugged.

"*¿Qué pasa?* What's wrong, son?"

"Nothing," I said quickly. "He's just tired of being inside all day." I glanced over at my brother still sitting on the floor.

"Oh, of course." Papá paused. "Perhaps not going outside at all *is* a bit drastic." Papá stooped down and tousled Frankie's hair. "I'll talk to your mother. I think playing in the yard would be fine."

"Fernando, I thought I heard you in here." Mamá joined us in Frankie's room. She'd put on lipstick and fixed her hair. It made me smile, how she always wanted to look nice when Papá came home.

"Sonia, I need to talk to you."

Mamá gave him a quick peck on the cheek. "Well, dinner is almost ready. . . ."

"It's important, but . . ." Papá gestured toward us.

Mamá nodded. "*Niños,* go downstairs and set the table for dinner."

"Do I have to?" Frankie asked.

"Frankie . . . ," Mamá answered.

He raised his hands in surrender. "I know, I know."

"And no nibbling on the *flan,*" Mamá warned as Frankie's stomping turned into a full sprint down the stairs.

"Lucy . . ." Papá looked at me.

I rolled my eyes. "I'm going, too."

Frankie's bedroom door closed behind me. I waited a moment, then pressed my ear against it.

"Well?" Mamá asked.

"It's the bank. They want me to be in charge—"

"A promotion! That's wonderful, what did Señor Betafil say?"

I breathed a sigh of relief. It wasn't Señor Betafil with the soldiers at the school. And if Papá got a promotion, that'd mean we could afford an even bigger *quinceañera* party in November. I smiled. Laura Milian was going to be so-o-o jealous.

"Sonia, that's the thing. . . . Betafil didn't give it to me. It came from Havana; they've taken Betafil into custody. They're holding him indefinitely. He . . ." Papá's voice trailed off.

It felt like someone had punched me in the stomach. I turned around and pressed my back against the door. *Señor Betafil was arrested?* My heart pounded. There was a ringing in my ears. I was going to be sick.

"Phone for you, Lucy," Frankie yelled from downstairs.

I didn't want to believe that the man I'd seen with the soldiers had been Papá's boss, but it had to be true. I needed to find out more. Who was that other man with Señor Betafil? Why were they there? What had they done? I put my ear to the door again, but now there were just hushed whispers. I felt stupid and selfish for thinking about my birthday party when so much was happening. I tried to convince myself that it didn't matter if I had a party at all. But part of me kept thinking that the soldiers might leave by November, so I could at least have a little celebration.

"Lucía! I'll hang up on your friend if you don't hurry up!" Frankie hollered, snapping me back to reality.

I ran downstairs and took the black receiver from Frankie's hand.

"Make it quick, 'cause I'm not setting the table by myself," Frankie warned.

I ignored him and said hello.

"Lucy, have I got some great *chisme* for you!" It was Ivette. "Can you talk? Do you feel better?"

I faked a small cough. "I'm still a little sick. What's the big gossip?"

"Well, I heard about it at the Jóvenes Rebeldes meeting."

"Since when do you go to *those* meetings? You've never been interested in politics. Aren't you the one who says it's more important to change your nail polish than change the government?"

Ivette laughed. "True, but my brothers were going, and since you were sick and I didn't have anything else to do . . ."

I winced. "Sorry."

"Oh no, it was great. There were lots of kids from

school and, ooh, so many good-looking boys! You have to come with me. We'll pick out a really nice outfit for you to wear."

"I don't know if I can go. Mamá worries about the soldiers and stuff."

"But these aren't soldiers . . . they're more like wannabe soldiers. You know, Manuel was there."

Just at the mention of his name, a smile spread across my face. "He was?"

"Yep, and he looked so cute, even in his *brigadista* uniform. He says he's leaving in a few weeks to go teach the peasants."

"Oh." My heart fell. I knew that the government was calling on all students over the age of thirteen to leave their families and go teach in the countryside for a few months, but no one I knew had actually signed up to go.

"Don't worry, he'll be back before your birthday party."

I tried to sound calm. "I wasn't even thinking about that."

"Ha! Don't act like you don't care. You're talking to *me*, remember? I've seen how you look at him."

My cheeks felt like they were on fire. "Do you think he knows?"

"Nah . . . well, maybe. He may have failed eighth grade, but he's still somewhat smart . . . for a boy. But don't worry about that. What about the meetings? You sure you can't go with me? My mother says everyone should go."

"Maybe in a few days. When my parents settle down a little."

"Yeah, I guess." Ivette sounded disappointed. "It's just boring not being able to gossip with anyone. The boys were cute, but the girls there had no sense of style. Most of them were wearing the ugly *brigadista* uniforms. Ugh."

I laughed. Ivette always had a way of making me feel better. "And you, Miss High Fashion, what were you wearing?"

"Are you kidding? I had this pretty yellow and white dress that matched my purse perfectly. No one says you can't rebel in style."

Ivette chuckled at her own joke.

"Ooh, and I almost forgot to tell you the *chisme*." Ivette lowered her voice. "Did you hear about Laura Milian's dad?"

"No, what?"

"Seems Little Miss Perfect's father got arrested last night in some big roundup. They picked up a bunch of anti-revolutionaries. Her father's such a lowlife. What a stupid *gusano*."

"What was he doing?"

"I heard that he was writing lies about Castro. You'd think after they shut down his precious newspaper he'd have learned his lesson. It was the talk of the meeting. They said—"

Frankie pulled on the phone cord. "Hang up. You've been talking for hours."

"Hold on, Ivette. Frankie's being a brat." I pushed him away.

"Mamá, Papá, Lucía isn't helping!" Frankie yelled from the bottom of the stairs. "Mamá! Papá!"

"Ivette, I gotta go. My parents think I'm setting the table, and Frankie's ratting me out."

"Okay, okay. Call me tomorrow. *¡Besos!*"

I hung up the phone and looked up toward Frankie's room. The door had remained shut. I wasn't sure if I wanted to know what they were still talking about.

Chapter 4

CRIME TO HAVE FOREIGN MONEY IN CUBA NOW
—*THE VALLEY INDEPENDENT*, MAY 6, 1961

After two full days of drenching spring storms, the darkest clouds parted and I began a campaign to recover my freedom.

"Please, Mamá, Frankie can go, too. We'll get groceries. Don't you need something? Anything?"

Mamá grabbed a pencil and began making a list.

I grinned. Finally, I was going to escape from house arrest.

"Okay, *vámonos.*" Mamá folded the paper and tucked it into her skirt pocket. "Call your brother."

"What? No, I meant I'd go for you, not with you." The moment I said it, I braced myself for a tongue-lashing. I could already hear the words. *¡Qué falta de respeto!* What disrespect!

Mamá simply raised an eyebrow and continued to fasten her light blue pillbox hat into place.

I followed as she walked to the hallway mirror to put on some lipstick. "Please, I need to be with my friends. What if they open up the schools tomorrow and I miss my chance to have fun? I can't take being cooped up anymore!"

"Lucía, *por favor*, it's barely been three days." She popped her lips together. "You act like you haven't seen them in months."

"It might as well be! You and Papá treat me like a baby! I'm fourteen. Kids my age are leaving home to join the revolution and you act like I'm still a little kid. Pretty soon you'll make me hold your hand when we cross the street!"

This time Mamá was not going to let it slide. She spun around. "Lucía, you watch your tone! I will not have you disrespecting me. When I was a child, I would never speak to my mother in that way. You have no idea what your father and I are going through."

I turned and rolled my eyes. What *they* were going through? What about me? My only consolation was knowing that someday I'd be free of all their stupid rules and worries.

"Frankie, let's go. We're going into town." Mamá pulled back the curtain, revealing the overcast sky. She took a deep breath. "I know you're upset, Lucía. Look, if we have time, we'll go by Machado's Pharmacy and see if they have any new fashion magazines."

I shrugged. I wasn't going to be bought off that easily. A trip to Machado's for a lollipop or paper dolls worked when I was a kid, but not anymore.

Frankie ran down the stairs, skipping the last two steps. "All right! We're finally out of here!"

Mamá smiled and grabbed her large bright-red umbrella and tucked it beneath her arm.

I hated that umbrella. It was like carrying a big stop sign that made everyone pause and take notice of us. A ridiculous umbrella for a ridiculous woman. Why couldn't she bring a plain black one? Why did she insist on embarrassing me with that thing?

"It's not even raining anymore," I said, and pointed outside.

"Well, just in case," she answered. *Mejor precaver que tener que lamentar."*

It was one of Mamá's favorite sayings . . . *Better safe than sorry.*

I followed her out the door. "Just because you've had that umbrella forever doesn't mean it's the only one you can use, you know."

"I like my umbrella. It's the only one I've ever found that's big enough to protect all of us from the rain," she said as Frankie jumped over the puddles lining the sidewalk.

"But red is the color of the revolution." I hoped this would make her reconsider.

Mamá stopped walking to look at me. "No, Lucía. The revolution may have taken over a lot of things, but it doesn't own a color. For me, red is the symbol of strength, and that's *all* it will ever represent."

❖   ❖   ❖   ❖   ❖

That evening, I begged Papá to let me join the Jóvenes Rebeldes. On our trip to town, I had noticed that the soldiers seemed to be everywhere. On every street corner, in every park. Despite what I'd seen and how nervous the soldiers made me feel, there was an intoxicating kind of energy that filled the air, cloaking everything. I even saw some classmates putting up flyers regarding the youth movement. They were laughing and waved to me, but Mamá ushered us along. I wanted to be with my friends. To be part of that excitement.

"Please, Papá, reconsider. Everyone is going."

Papá shook his head. "Why can't you invite your friends over to the house and listen to music like before?" He leaned back in his favorite chair and unfolded the evening paper.

I read the headline at the top of the page: *Apoya la CTC la Nacionalización de las Escuelas Privadas.* I thought about it for a few seconds. Maybe I could use the fact that Cuba's labor union was supporting the nationalization of all the private schools to convince

Papá that going to the meetings was okay. Show him that the school closings were nothing to worry about.

I placed my hand on his arm. Ivette had explained that some parents were afraid of change and that it was up to us to lead the way. "Papá, look." I pointed to the headline. "The schools will open again, and everyone will think it's strange that I don't go to the meetings." I used my most serious voice. "It's important."

He took his reading glasses from the coffee table and slid them over his nose. "Doesn't matter what others think." He popped open the newspaper. "And the private schools won't open again, only the ones run by the revolution. A revolution my daughter is not getting involved with."

"But why?"

"Lucy, you're just too young," he said, staring at the newspaper.

"The revolution doesn't think I'm too young. See." I pointed to a picture of teenagers waving from a train that was headed to the brigades' camp in Varadero. "Thousands of kids my age and younger have joined the brigades. *Their* parents trust them."

Papá slapped the side of the chair with the newspaper as if swatting an imaginary fly. "It's not about trust. Don't you realize that they're *having* to leave their homes for months to go teach and live in the mountains?

How it's now expected that all *good revolutionaries* will send their kids to the brigades? Is that what you want? To be by yourself in a new place?"

"Better than being stuck here," I muttered.

"You think your mother and I enjoy saying no to you? We only want the best for you, to protect you. *They* don't care about breaking up families. It's actually what they want. To destroy the family so the only thing left is the revolution, just like Karl Marx suggested." Papá shook his head. "And this so-called revolution continues to go after anyone who dares to think. To disagree." Papá sighed. "Lucy, it's just so complicated . . ."

"It's complicated because you and Mamá don't understand that I've grown up!" Tears rose in my eyes. One blink and they'd land on my cheeks. "You are so unfair!" I turned and raced up the stairs. I slammed my bedroom door and felt a scream rise up in my chest. Now I understood why the soldiers got so angry. People like my father couldn't see that the younger generation wanted Cuba to change for the better. They didn't see all the good things that the revolution could do. He's so stubborn, I thought. Why can't he be like Ivette's father?

I caught my breath as I heard Papá coming up the stairs. I didn't want to confront him again. My heart beat faster. I'd never raised my voice at him before. The footsteps stopped right outside my door. After a few seconds, I heard them continue down the hall.

I slowly exhaled.

Stupid *gusano.*

* * * * *

The smell of onions and garlic brought me down to dinner. As much as I didn't want to see Papá, I figured maybe my mother could reason with him.

"*Mi hija,* can you get the glasses, please?" Mamá took out a starched linen tablecloth and snapped it open over the kitchen table.

I walked past the open kitchen window and took the glasses from the cupboard. "Mamá you'll let me go to a Jóvenes meeting with Ivette, right?"

She shook her head. "Don't try playing me against your father. I know he doesn't want you going."

I set the glasses down and reached into the kitchen drawer to take out the silverware. "But . . ."

"There's no need for you to get involved with the revolution . . . it won't last. It never does. I've seen Cuba go through so many leaders, all of them with their promises. Each of them just as corrupt as the one before."

"Yeah, but this time it's different. You know that."

"I know that this revolution is jailing good people. That decent, God-loving priests and nuns are being kicked out just because they dare to voice their concerns about what's going on. Different is not always a good thing." Mamá went to the stove to flip over the *palomilla* steaks. "Plus, now that your father is running the bank, he hears things."

"Like what?"

"Like the fact that Ivette's mother is involved with the CDR," Papá said as he walked into the kitchen and took his seat at the head of the table.

"Hmm, the Committee for the Defense of the Revolution . . . now it makes sense," Mamá muttered.

Papá flashed her a strange look.

"No, Fernando, nothing bad. She called me this morning to ask why we weren't more involved with the revolution. She said we seemed 'suspicious.' She suggested I send Lucía to the Jóvenes meetings and that Frankie go to the Pioneros group . . . so we could show our loyalty."

Papá shook his head. "Who do we have to prove anything to?"

"Maybe I should join something, just so that there isn't talk," Mamá offered.

"No, Sonia. We do what is required and that's it. But we need to be careful with that family; the CDR are glorified neighborhood spies."

I couldn't believe how judgmental Papá was being. I'd read the newspapers and knew how much the revolution wanted to help people. It said that the factories had been closed because the owners were giving all their profits to foreigners and that the churches had been infiltrated by American sympathizers. Castro had no choice but to have the government take over many of the businesses so that there wouldn't be so much corruption. It was all for the benefit of the country, and everyone was expected to pitch in and help. What harm was there in that? Even if I didn't agree with what had happened with Señor Betafil, so many smart people supported the revolution, they couldn't all be wrong. "Not all of the CDR are bad. Tío Antonio joined—"

Papá pushed back his chair. "Antonio joined the CDR? Who told you this?"

My heart raced. I couldn't tell him it was Ivette. Then they'd really dislike her family.

Mamá spoke up. "It's true. Antonio came by yesterday and told me. Lucía probably overheard us talking. And yes, I was surprised, too, but you know your brother would never do anything to hurt us."

"And Ivette wouldn't hurt us, either. We've been friends forever, and you've known her parents for years."

"The revolution has changed people. It's not just the soldiers we have to be worried about," Papá said.

"But he's your brother. He's the only family we have left." Mamá placed her hand on Papá's shoulder as she set down a platter of yellow rice.

"*No importa*. In fact, I think it's better if you don't talk so much with Ivette, either, Lucy."

"What?" I couldn't believe what he was saying.

"You're not serious. She's my best friend. Her mother only called because I said you wouldn't let me go to the meetings. She was just trying to help."

"Humpf." Papá pointed to the smoke starting to rise from the stove. "Sonia, I think the steaks are burning."

"*¡Ay Dios!*" Mamá quickly pulled the sizzling pan away from the open flame.

Papá turned to face me again, his face softer. "*Mi hija,* it's not just Ivette's mother. Her father came by the bank today to remind me of my duty to the revolution to report anything suspicious."

"So?" I shrugged.

Papá paused. "You really don't see it?" He shook his head. "Of course not, most of the people around here don't see the problem, either. Everyone's in love with all the fancy rhetoric." He ran his fingers through his hair. "What he meant was that he wants me to spy on the bank employees and the customers. He even mentioned how much he'd hate to see anything happen to me or my new promotion." Papá's face started to turn red. "That it would be a shame if, because of a silly misunderstanding, I were classified as an anti-revolutionary and sent to prison like Betafil." Papá stood and paced around the kitchen. "It was a threat. That good-for-nothing thinks he has power now. A year ago, he was nothing more than a lazy salesman in a shoe store, and today he wants to dictate my code of ethics. I'm telling you, this revolution is *una mentira*. It's all a bunch of lies."

"Fernando, please. Someone might hear." Mamá ran to close the kitchen window.

"What? I can't even speak my mind in my own house without worrying that a neighbor is listening. This is becoming absurd! Lucía, you will not go to those meetings and that's final!" Papá slung open the back door. "Sonia, I need some fresh air. Go ahead and eat without me." He stormed out, not even bothering to close the door behind him.

My heart beat wildly, but I sat frozen in my chair. I'd never seen Papá so angry. I glanced over at Mamá, who stood by the sink picking imaginary crumbs from her apron. She then rolled back her shoulders and walked to the stove.

"Close the door and call your brother to dinner," she said in a quiet voice.

I shut the door and walked to the living room looking for Frankie. As I stood by the large picture window in the front of the house, I caught a glimpse of Papá's silhouette. He was crossing the street, and the light from the streetlamps elongated his shadow against the wide sidewalk. A quick movement, glimpsed out of the corner of my eye, made me look away from him. At first, I wasn't sure what it was. Then it happened again a little farther down the block. Even in the fading twilight, I could see window curtains being pulled slightly open, and then, as Papá walked by, they were abruptly closed again. It was almost like . . . we were being watched.

Chapter 5

I flipped through an old *Seventeen* magazine for the umpteenth time while I listened to one of my favorite Elvis records. Reading the articles about other teenage girls was one of the few benefits I could see to having taken English for so many years in school. I wished I could read a new issue, but with all of Cuba's problems with the U.S., there was little chance I'd be seeing any new American magazines at the pharmacy.

The sound of the doorbell broke up the monotony of the day. I tossed aside the magazine and ran downstairs.

"*¿Quién es?*" I asked at the door.

"*Soy yo, Ivette.*"

Quickly I unlocked the door and pulled my friend inside. "Thank God you're here!" I hugged her. "Mamá and Papá have been driving me crazy!"

Ivette smiled. "I don't know how you've survived." She grabbed my hand and twirled me around. "And look at you . . . a week without me and you've let yourself go! No ribbon around your ponytail and your nails aren't even painted!" she teased. "We need to do something about this."

"Yes, please! Save me!" I giggled.

"Lucía, who is it?" Mamá asked from the back porch.

"It's Ivette! We're going to my room!" I pushed Ivette up the stairs. I wasn't sure how Mamá would react to having Ivette here, but I wasn't going to take any chances.

"What's gotten into you? I didn't even get a chance to say hello to your mother." Ivette plopped herself down on my bed.

"Forget her. Let's talk about more important things, like what you've been up to."

Ivette rummaged through the box of records that sat next to my night table. "Nothing, other than Jóvenes meetings. Here, put this one on." She gave me a record by Celia Cruz. "And since you don't want to join us, maybe I shouldn't tell you what happened today."

"You know it's not my choice." I placed the record-player arm gently on the small forty-five. Music filled the room again. "I'd go if I could."

Ivette smiled. "Yeah, I know. I'm just teasing. And that's exactly what Carmen was today. A big tease. She spent the whole time trying to flirt with Manuel, but he didn't seem to care. Trust me, she's no competition for you."

"Have people asked about me?" I picked at my chipped nail polish.

"People? You mean has Manuel asked?" Ivette leaned back on the bed, her body moving in rhythm with the song's mix of bongo drums and the distinct hollow sound of the *claves*. "Well, I mentioned that I was coming over, and he said to make sure to tell you about the dance that Jóvenes is sponsoring at the end of the month. It's a party for everyone who is volunteering to work with the brigades in the countryside. I think he wants to find an excuse to see you before he goes."

"Really?" I studied her face to make sure she was being serious. Just the thought of dancing with Manuel was enough to make my stomach do a flip.

Ivette nodded.

"Ooh," I squealed, and jumped up. I ran over to my closet and threw open the doors. "What should I wear? You have to help me pick something out."

"You sure you can go?"

I pulled out a pink flowered dress and draped it in front of me. I spun around to face her. "Oh, I'm going, just watch me!"

❀   ❀   ❀   ❀   ❀

For the next couple of weeks, I did everything my parents asked without bringing up the Jóvenes meetings. From time to time, Ivette would come over and we'd listen to music. She reassured me that eventually my parents would get used to the soldiers. She said it was like walking into a kitchen after something had burned. At first, the odor almost knocks you over, but after a while, you forget there was ever a bad smell. I could tell this was already happening with Mamá since I was now allowed to go into town by myself to do quick errands.

Finally, the timing was perfect to bring up the dance. I'd caught Mamá humming while she folded some of the laundry.

"Mamá, can I talk to you about something?"

"Of course." Mamá put aside the clothes that needed to be ironed.

I twisted a long strand of hair around my finger. "I know I'm not supposed to date until I'm sixteen, but I'm allowed to go to dances, right?"

Mamá stopped, looked at me, and smiled. "Well, I suppose so . . . with a chaperone, of course."

I decided to take the plunge. "Mamá, a bunch of my friends are going to a dance at the Yacht Club this Saturday. I want to go. There'll be a bunch of chaperones there."

"That's only four days away. Plus, I thought the government closed down the Yacht Club. Called it a symbol of the elite."

"Yeah, but it reopened as a cultural center. Anyone can go there now."

Mamá started folding one of Papá's undershirts.

"Humpf, doubt that. If you're not an 'appropriate revolutionary' they won't let you in. Anyone who dares to disagree with Che or Fidel can't keep their job, let alone go to a social function." She picked up another shirt. "But I do remember going to parties there when I was your age. Abuela used to sit in the corner with all the other mothers." Mamá clutched the shirt against her chest. She had a faraway look in her eyes. "I guess it's my turn to chaperone you now."

"So is that a yes?" I wanted to bounce up and down. I didn't care if Mamá was going to be there too. I was going to dance with Manuel!

"I don't see why—"

Papá stormed into the room. "Where's my hammer?"

Mamá and I both jumped. "Fernando, you scared us to death! What are you doing here in the middle of the day?"

"My hammer, where is it?" Papá yanked open a drawer in the cabinet next to the sofa. "This'll do." He took out a flat-edge screwdriver.

"Fernando, *¿qué pasó?* What has you like this?"

Papá looked at Mamá's worried face and took a deep breath.

"Nothing, Sonia. Don't worry. I just don't have much time. I have to get back to the office right away." Papá glanced over at me. "Can you go upstairs and make sure your brother isn't getting into too much trouble?"

"Sure," I muttered. I'd become used to my parents' behind-closed-doors conversations. After going up the first few steps, I stopped and crouched down in the stairway. From that vantage point, I couldn't be seen, but I could still watch and hear a little of what was happening.

Papá moved the wooden coffee table, lifted up the rug, and tapped the tiles underneath with the back of the screwdriver. One of the taps sounded more hollow than all the others. Papá immediately began chiseling around the tile.

"Fernando, *por favor*, what's going on? Tell me."

Papá wouldn't stop chiseling. "Sonia, they've announced that citizens can no longer have any holdings. The government is confiscating everything." Papá lifted up the tile and placed it onto the rolled-up rug. "Look at this. Me, a banker, hiding money underneath my home because I can't trust my own bank." Papá pulled out a bunch of papers from the hole in the floor and waved them in the air. "All our savings in stocks . . . useless! Now not only are we limited to how much money we can legally have, we can't even own shares in corporations!" Papá emptied his wallet and shoved some cash into the floor.

"But they can't do that, can they? Just take it away? We're investors in those businesses."

Papá shook his head. "They can and they are."

"Still, we should keep those papers. Things might change."

"Ha!" He threw the stock certificates back into the hole. "I'll keep them just in case, but I'm telling you, they'll only be reminders of what we once had. What I did do is empty out our safe-deposit box." Papá put his hand in his coat pocket and pulled out a handful of jewelry. "Your mother's ring, my father's watch, everything." Papá shook his head. "The idea is that all the wealth should be spread out. So they're taking from those who have worked their entire lives, like us, keeping some of the money for themselves and then supposedly giving the rest to the poor. Isn't that wonderful? I've worked since I was fifteen just so I can be as poor as the bum who never worked a day in his life. Welcome to Castro's revolution!"

"Fernando, it can't be that bad. And having those things here? They could get stolen." Mamá wrung her hands together.

"Greater chance of it being taken at the bank." Papá wrapped the jewelry in his handkerchief and placed it into the hole. He put back the loose tile and tapped it down. "Sonia, I need you to go upstairs and get me a couple of pieces of jewelry that you don't care about. Just in case they check on our box, I want to have something in there."

Frankie came out of his room and I motioned for him to be quiet. He joined me on the stairs and we both listened together.

"Fernando, isn't this a bit much? Why would they be interested in us?"

"Sonia, don't you see? This revolution is all about control. They're watching me, you, everybody. The soldiers are monitoring everything at the bank. Who comes in, who takes what. They're going after anyone they think is a threat. I'm not taking sides on any of the issues, but even that could be considered traitorous. I was able to get these things only because a few of us worked together. It felt like I was stealing, and it's my own property! You have to trust me."

I watched as Mamá gently stroked the side of Papá's face. "I do trust you. I'll get you the jewelry. Should we hide these, too?" She pointed to the small diamond earrings she was wearing.

Papá covered her hands with his own. "No, those were your grandmother's. You've worn them since we met. Too many things have changed around here. I don't want you to change, too." He pulled Mamá into his arms.

"Ugh, yuck!" Frankie whispered, and returned to his room.

I sat back and tried to absorb everything I'd witnessed. The newspapers had stories about people hoarding money and property. They accused these people of being greedy anti-revolutionaries. I'd read how the revolution wanted the working class to save their money. It was only the lazy rich who had to share with those who had less. So why was Papá so worried? We certainly weren't rich. Plus, Papá had worked hard every day of his life, and although he wasn't a fan of the revolution, he most definitely wasn't an anti-revolutionary. No one could really fault him for trying to protect what was ours. Could they?

Chapter 6

CASTRO HOLDS LIFE CHEAP
—*THE CHARLESTON GAZETTE*, MAY 25, 1961

"Lucía, Frankie woke up with a fever." Mamá poked her head into my room. "I need you to go pick up some medicine for him at Machado's Pharmacy."

I was just about to complain about being woken up when her words made it all the way to my brain. During the last few weeks, errands had been my only way out of the house. "*Está bien*, Mamá. I'll be ready in *cinco minutos*."

I quickly jumped out of bed, grabbed some clothes, pulled my hair into a ponytail, and gave myself a light spritz of perfume. "I'm ready!" I yelled before Mamá had a chance to change her mind.

Mamá waited for me by the front door. "Just go to the pharmacy and come straight home. No side trips to Ivette's or anywhere else, understand?"

I nodded as she handed me some money.

"I've given you enough for some baby aspirin and camphor, but there's a little extra there, too."

"Uh-huh." I tapped my foot, eager to leave. Running errands had never been high on my list of fun things to do, but at least it gave me a chance to breathe some fresh air and get away from Mamá's watchful eye. Plus, there was a chance I'd run into some friends along the way.

"You can buy yourself a pretty nail polish or some face powder." Mamá fought back a smile.

"Okay, sure." Did she expect me to jump for joy over face powder? If I were allowed to cut my hair short or wear makeup, then maybe . . .

A huge smile broke out across Mamá's face. "You'll want to look nice for the dance on Saturday."

It took a moment to sink in. I couldn't believe it . . . she was going to let me go! I threw my arms around her neck. "Thank you, Mamá, thank you!"

She squeezed me back. "I spoke with your father last night. You deserve to have a little fun. You *are* fourteen; we've got to let you grow up a little." She pulled away and looked me straight in the eye. "But I'll be there chaperoning."

I did a little dance in the doorway. "That's okay." I jumped up and down. "I love you so much!"

"Well, thank your father, too, when he gets home. But now I need that medicine, so go!"

I turned and skipped to the sidewalk. It felt like I could float all the way to town. When I finally reached Machado's Pharmacy, I headed straight for the cosmetics counter, where Doc Machado's sister, Señora Garra, sat on a stool facing the front window.

"*Buenos días*, Señora Garra."

Señora Garra spun around to face me. "Oh, Lucía, what can I do for you?"

"I'd like a bottle of Mademoiselle Pink nail polish." It was a color I'd seen advertised in one of my fashion magazines.

Señora Garra's attention went to the front door as someone else came inside. She glanced over at me and gave me a slight smile. "*Perdóname*, what did you ask me for?"

"Mademoiselle Pink polish."

Señora Garra stole another glimpse at the door.

"Is everything okay?" I asked.

"*Sí, sí*. Machado's just running a little late this morning. As for the polish, we haven't had that in a while. But we do have some other very nice shades of light pink. Is this for anything special?"

I looked down and felt my cheeks get warm. "Um, for a dance." I wasn't sure why I was embarrassed to say this out loud.

"Oh my! I can't believe it!" She shook her head. "Seems like only yesterday you were in a baby carriage." She held up one finger and eased off the metal stool. "I have one bottle left of a color that'll be just perfect for you. It's a little more red than what you were asking for, but it's just right for a young lady growing up." She bent down, took a small bottle off the bottom shelf, and placed it on the glass countertop.

It was a light berry-colored polish. Perfect for the dress I planned on wearing.

"I'll take it!"

"Anything else you need?"

"Children's aspirin and camphor."

Señora Garra peeked out the store window. "Somebody sick?"

"Frankie has a bad cold." I opened the little bottle and put a drop on my fingernail. The color made me feel glamorous. I'd fix my nails the moment I got home.

Señora Garra walked back over with a small brown bag and dropped the polish inside. "Hope Frankie feels better. Tell your mother to call if she needs to speak to Doc Machado. I'm sure he'll be here any minute."

I nodded, paid, and left the pharmacy with dreams of dancing with Manuel.

The rumbling of the cars passing by, the hum of conversations too distant to really understand, and the jingle of bells as people entered stores created a rhythm that soon became the soundtrack to the dance I was imagining. Manuel would have his hand on my back and we'd glide around the dance floor like in the movies. He'd look into my eyes and whisper how I was the most beautiful girl he'd ever seen. Then the music would end and he'd continue holding my hand for the rest of the night.

As I rounded the first corner and passed the hardware store, I peeked inside the bag to take another look at my purchase. That's when I smacked right into Laura Milian.

"Lucía!" She turned our collision into a light hug. "It's so good to see you!"

"Oh." I was surprised she was even talking to me. "Hi."

"What have you been up to lately?"

"Me?" I shrugged. "Nothing much."

"Yeah, me neither." She smiled. "Guess we have a lot in common nowadays, huh?"

I gave her a blank stare. Laura Milian and I had nothing in common. She was queen of the popular crowd and I, well, I had Ivette.

She lowered her voice and gave me a little nudge with her elbow. "You know what I mean. People not really talking to us anymore because we don't go to the Jóvenes meetings and all."

I remembered that Ivette had told me that Laura's father had been arrested for spreading anti-revolutionary lies. That was probably why her friends had all stopped talking to her. "No, that's not really happening to me."

Laura looked surprised. "Oh. Well, anyway, it's nice to talk to you. Are you going shopping or something?"

"No, I'm on my way home. I had to run a quick errand." I felt the shape of the bottle in the bag. Laura would probably think it was silly or unfashionable. I decided not to show her.

"Oh well. Maybe we can do something later. I know we've never hung out or anything, but things are different now and I thought, maybe . . ."

I had to admit, I liked the idea that one of the coolest girls in school wanted to be my friend. Then again, she was now a former popular kid, which was probably the only reason she was talking to me. *Plato de segunda mesa,* as my mother would say. "I don't know. My parents aren't really letting me do much."

Laura's face fell.

I could see the disappointment in her eyes. I'd always had Ivette to count on, but she didn't seem to have anyone left. "Well, maybe one of these afternoons or something," I offered.

"Okay." She perked up. "Hey, you said you're going home, right?"

I nodded.

Laura got a little closer to me. "I wouldn't go down Central Avenue. Something was happening over there a few minutes ago. There were a ton of soldiers, and that many of them can't be good. I think . . ." She paused as an old man passed by us. "Just be careful."

"Sure." I glanced down at my watch. "My mother's waiting. I've got to get going."

"Oh, right. We'll talk soon, okay?"

"Mmm-hmm," I said, and turned to head home.

It was strange the way Laura was speaking before that old man walked by us. A bit overly dramatic and, like my parents, a little too paranoid for my taste. I shook the thoughts about Laura Milian away and concentrated on Manuel again. I glanced at the little spot of reddish pink on my nail. The color seemed to sparkle under the dazzling morning sun.

I crossed the street, opened the pharmacy bag, and pulled out the polish. I held it up, admiring the truly perfect shade. I was going to look so pretty. I couldn't wait to tell Ivette that I'd be able to go with her to the dance. She'd be so happy for me.

By the time I passed the old courthouse, with its large front steps rising to meet the columns near the front doors, I realized I'd been walking down Central Avenue. It was the way I always went home, but Laura had said there were a lot of soldiers in the area.

I spun around.

The street was empty . . . too empty.

My heart raced.

Where were all the soldiers? Where was . . . anyone? Either Laura had lied or something was very wrong.

I saw the city park up ahead. I could cut through there, cross over to José Martí Boulevard, and get home that way.

I closed my fist over the bottle and ran down the large tree-lined promenade. My eyes focused on the flowered park entrance. I made a sharp turn past the blooming azaleas and stopped short.

I gasped in horror.

There, from the oak tree on the corner, hung the body of Doc Machado! A scream escaped from the back of my throat and I dropped the little bottle. It shattered against the sidewalk, leaving a pool of red next to my shoes.

I didn't know what to do. My heart beat so loudly I couldn't think. I wanted to fall down, but my legs wouldn't bend.

A police car drove by slowly . . . watching.

The next thing I knew, I was running. I didn't know where I was headed until I saw Papá's bank in front of me. I wanted to run inside and have him hold me in his arms, but something made me pause. I inched toward the large front window and peered inside. Papá sat at his desk, calmly talking with a few soldiers. I turned and leaned against the glass. A group of young *brigadistas* walked by, laughing. There seemed to be soldiers, or kids pretending to be soldiers, everywhere. I took a deep breath, got my bearings, and took off running again. This time, I didn't stop until I was home.

Chapter 7

THREE INVADERS FACE CASTRO FIRING SQUAD
—*THE SALINA JOURNAL*, MAY 25, 1961

"Lucía? I'm upstairs. Do you have the medicine?" Mamá called out as the front door slammed behind me.

I ran to my parents' room, dropped the brown paper bag on the bed, and plowed my head into Mamá's chest, nearly knocking her over.

"What's wrong? Why are you out of breath?" Mamá asked.

I started to cry.

"Tell me, Lucía."

The words didn't seem to want to come out of my mouth. I shook my head.

Mamá stroked my hair and let me sob in her arms. After a few minutes, she pushed me back and stared into my eyes. *"Mi hija,* talk. You're scaring me." She scanned me from head to toe. "Wait, I think I see what this is about." She lifted my chin so I'd have to face her.

I waited, praying that she already knew what had happened.

"Is this about the nail polish?"

My heart sank. She had no idea. I looked down as my eyes welled up. The image of Doc Machado with his hands hanging lifeless by his side haunted me.

Mamá smiled and kissed my forehead. "*Mi hija,* look at your shoes. They're splattered with bright red dots. You dropped the bottle on your way home, didn't you?"

I nodded.

She got up from her bed and smoothed out the wrinkles in her skirt. "It'll be fine. I have a little extra money in my purse. You can go back and—"

"NO!"

"Lucía, what's gotten into you? Did something else happen?"

"Mamá, Doc Machado, he's . . ." I couldn't continue.

"*¿Qué?*" She drew closer.

I gulped for air. My hands trembled. "He's . . . dead. The soldiers, they killed him."

Mamá stumbled back. "*¡Ay Dios mío!*" She quickly made the sign of the cross.

Then, like a floodgate opening up, words spilled out of me. "Oh, Mamá, he was hung from a tree. *I saw him.* They left him there, in the park, for everyone to see. It was horrible!"

Mamá rushed over to sit next to me. "But the soldiers didn't do anything to you, right?"

I shook my head and buried my face in her chest.

Mamá wrapped her arms around me as my body collapsed. All the adrenaline that had rushed through me evaporated. Suddenly I was exhausted. I closed my eyes and breathed in Mamá's warmth. "I'm never leaving this house again," I sobbed.

❀   ❀   ❀   ❀   ❀

"Are you sick, too?" Frankie asked, walking into my room.

"Go away." I rolled over and pulled the covers up to my neck, trying to go back to sleep.

"Did you get my cold? You want to play something together?"

"Get out!"

Mamá promptly appeared in the doorway and guided Frankie back to his room.

"But, Mamá, I didn't say anything wrong. She's been in there all day!" Frankie argued.

"You, sir, get back in bed. You've got a high fever and you need your rest." She gave him a slight push into his room and then came back to me. "Lucy, how are you doing? You want to eat something? I can bring your dinner upstairs along with Frankie's."

I shook my head.

"Lucy, I called your father and told him what happened. He'll be here soon. He wants to talk to both of us." Mamá tucked a tear-soaked strand of hair behind my ear.

I nodded, knowing that at home I was safe. I sat up in my bed and looked outside as the sun began to set. This awful day was almost over, and once Papá arrived, everything would get better . . . somehow.

"Lucía! Sonia!" Papá called out.

"*Aquí*, Fernando. In Lucía's room."

Papá walked into the room and knelt by my bed. He took my hand and gave it a kiss. "Oh, Lucy, how I wish you'd been spared from seeing . . ."

I nodded, not wanting to think or talk about what I'd seen.

"Why, Fernando? Why'd they do it?" Mamá stood and walked toward the window.

Papá placed my hand against his cheek. "To set an example. Scare anyone who might think of going against the revolution."

Mamá shook her head and played with one of her diamond earrings. "He was a pharmacist, for heaven's sake," she muttered, "not a threat to anyone."

Papá looked back toward her. "They don't care. A dialogue. That's all he wanted. He was organizing a group to talk about some of the changes being made, the rights being taken away that he felt weren't in keeping with the original ideals of the revolution. He wanted a simple, peaceful protest to give voice to what so many feel is a betrayal of what the revolution was supposed to do. But that was too much for them. *¡Cobardes!*"

A giant lump formed in my throat at the thought of Papá doing something against the government. "Papá, promise me that you'll never do anything like that . . . ever. Please!"

He turned to face me again, his eyes moist with tears. "Don't worry, Lucy. Nothing is going to happen to me or to any of us. I'll do anything to protect this family. But I need—"

"Hi, Papá." Frankie trudged into the room.

"Come here, *mi hijo*. How do you feel?" Papá picked Frankie up and gave him a hug.

"Mamá says I have a fever."

"I know." He carried Frankie over to my bed and sat next to him. "But you feel good enough to listen to some important things I have to say. Right, little man?"

Frankie nodded. I could see how much he loved to be included in family discussions.

"I was just going to tell your mother and sister that, from now on, I want all of us to sit outside on the porch, every evening. It'll show that we have nothing to hide from the CDR. We'll smile and act like everything is fine."

"Isn't everything fine?" Frankie asked.

"Of course it is," Mamá answered.

Papá shook his head. "No, Frankie, everything isn't

fine"—he reached out and grabbed Mamá's hand—"but it will be."

Mamá's shoulders seemed to drop a little and she smiled.

"I still don't like the idea of either of you going to any meetings, but otherwise we're going to do everything else our neighbors do," Papá continued. "And, Lucy, going to the dance on Saturday will help, too."

"But I don't want to go anymore," I said.

Papá pulled me toward him and gave me a kiss on the top of my head. "You have to, Lucy. We need to show that we're not keeping you away from the revolution."

"Fernando, if she doesn't want to, is it really that important? She's been through a lot."

"I wouldn't ask if it wasn't needed." Papá stood up. He paced around the room rubbing his temples. "Sonia, you should know that an army captain came by the bank today. He mentioned that he was surprised to hear that my children weren't involved with the Jóvenes Rebeldes or Los Pioneros. He insinuated that if I couldn't teach my children how to be good revolutionaries, then maybe the government should take on that responsibility."

Mamá covered her mouth. "You don't think the rumors are true, do you, Fernando?"

"What rumors?" I asked, looking at my parents to try to understand the coded language they were speaking.

Papá ignored my question. "I don't know if it's true.

Eduardo at the bank swears that his brother saw a document with a government seal on it discussing *patria potestad*. But who knows?"

"*Patria potes*-what?" I asked, sitting up straight in bed.

"Yeah, what is that?" Frankie asked.

"*Nada*," Mamá said. "Nothing either of you has to worry about. Fernando, let's talk about this later, but Lucía, your father is right. We need you—"

"I know." I sighed. "I need to go to the dance."

Chapter 8

POLLS INDICATE CASTRO WILL SOON GO TOO FAR
—*THE PROGRESS*, MAY 26, 1961

"*¡Levántate!* Look what time it is." Mamá threw open my bedroom curtains.

"Ugh." I put the pillow over my face. Mamá's famous chamomile tea with *tilo* and *anís* had helped me go to sleep even though I was convinced I'd only have nightmares.

"Let's see what you plan on wearing tomorrow night," she said.

I peeled off the pillow and squinted as my eyes adjusted to the room's brightness. Did she think I could forget about what happened yesterday?

"*¿Qué te vas a poner?* Maybe you can wear that pretty yellow one that you wore to Camila Renderon's wedding a few months ago."

I shook my head and pointed to the pink dress

with the white eyelet trim hanging on the door of the closet.

"*Ah sí, bien lindo*. Did you try it on to make sure it still fits?" Mamá walked over to check the hem.

"It's fine," I muttered. There was nothing she could say to make me feel better. I was only going to do this because we needed to keep up appearances.

"No, better let me see it on. I can let out the bottom another inch or so. You've grown since you wore it during Christmas."

I sat up in my bed. "Mamá, dresses are worn shorter, anyway."

"Just try it on. Then we'll decide. How about shoes? You're almost the same size as me. You want to wear my pink heels? They're not too high, and I think they'd look nice with the dress."

I smiled at the thought of Manuel seeing me in my best dress and pink heels. I'd look so grown-up. I stretched and walked over to the mirror.

"Yeah, I guess the heels would be good. What about my hair?" I picked it up into a French twist and looked at myself from different angles.

"Hmm, sounds like a question for Ivette." She paused for a moment. "Better ask her when she gets here in a few minutes. I invited her and her **mother** over for lunch."

I let my hair drop as I spun around. "She is? You did?"

Mamá nodded. "A girl can't plan for her first dance without her best friend. Plus, I need to mend some fences."

I tackled my mother with a huge bear hug. Everything *was* getting better.

❄ ❄ ❄ ❄ ❄

"*Chica*, you don't look too happy. I thought you'd be more excited about going to the dance."

Ivette grabbed a nail file from my dresser.

"I am happy."

"Yeah, sure. You had that fake smile all during lunch. You'd think we were about to take one of Señora Cardoza's final exams or something." Ivette plopped onto my bed. "You're going to get to dance with Manuel. You should be on cloud nine. This is *the* Manuel. Boy of your dreams, remember?"

"I know. I *am* excited." I flashed a smile so exaggerated that my face hurt. "See?"

"Better not smile like that. Manuel's gonna think you've gone crazy or something."

I opened the bottom drawer of my dresser and started organizing the socks and silk scarves inside. "He may not even want to dance with me. I might just sit there all night."

"*Ay*, you are in a mood!" Ivette stopped filing her nail and looked at me. "I know for a fact that Manuel wants to dance with you before he leaves on Monday."

"How can you? You're not a mind reader."

"No, but Raúl asked me if you were going."

"So? Why would your brother care?" I continued folding a yellow and blue scarf.

"Let me finish." She blew the dust off her fingernails. "Raúl asked me because . . ." Her eyes twinkled.

Something was up. Ivette really did know something. "¿*Por qué?* Tell me!"

She bounced on the bed. "He asked because his best friend, Enrique, said his cousin only wants to go to the dance if you're going. And you know Enrique's cousin is . . ."

"Manuel!" I squealed and sprang up off the floor.

Ivette giggled. "Okay, that's more like it. This is the Lucía I know!"

I jumped on the bed next to her. "Is Manuel really leaving on Monday?"

"*Sí.* He's all excited. My brother's going, too."

"He is? Aren't your parents worried? Him being by himself and everything?"

Ivette looked down at my pink bedspread and started twirling a snagged piece of string stuck to one of the corners. "There isn't too much to worry about. It's very organized and it's for the revolution. Teaching the peasants to read with all the other *brigadistas*. My parents say all students should spend some of their time doing that since they've had the privilege of receiving a good education in the cities." Ivette shrugged. "I don't really care about the teaching, but the traveling to other places, meeting new people . . . that part does sound pretty cool. It's not Paris or Rome, but it's a start."

"I guess." I didn't want to talk or even think about the revolution. "So, what did you decide to wear to the dance?"

"Ooh, my mother bought me this white dress with little black polka dots. It's got a patent-leather belt around the waist. It makes me look like I'm at least seventeen. Very ooh-la-la sophisticated!"

"A new dress, huh?" I wiggled my fingers at her. "Well, aren't we fancy!" I laughed. "People might confuse you with one of the rich girls."

Ivette gave me a smirk. "Ha, ha. I guess Papá's new job with the government does have some perks. Plus, it's kind of a gift before I . . ." She bit her bottom lip.

"Before what?"

Ivette searched my eyes. "Nothing," she said, and looked away.

"Ivette, what's going on?"

"*Nada*. I got the dress because it's my first real dance, that's all." She rolled off the bed and opened my top drawer.

"Are you sure? Is there something else?"

"Nope. Nothing else to say except . . . what jewelry are you going to wear?"

I shrugged. "You're the expert. What do you think?"

Ivette dug into my wooden jewelry box and pulled

out a gold chain with a white daisy on it. "Well, this just screams out 'I'm a little girl,' so forget this one." Next, she picked out a silver necklace with a small cross. "Oh no. We can't make you holy and untouchable. You'll never get your first kiss that way."

I blushed and nervously started to giggle.

"Can you picture it?" She draped the chain around her neck and swayed to imaginary music. "Hi, Manuel. Oh, of course I'd like to dance, but be careful if you hold me too close, because not only is my mother chaperoning, God is watching and you'll be sent straight to hell." Ivette couldn't hold back her laughter. "No, this is definitely not the right necklace!"

I threw a pillow across the room and hit her in the arm. "You're terrible!"

"Who, me?" Ivette dropped the chain back in the drawer. "Let's ask your mom if we can borrow something. I'm sure she's got something nice. I mean, this is like a dress rehearsal for our *quinces*."

I thought about how Papá had hidden all the good jewelry under the loose tile in the living room. "No. We can't."

She gave me a puzzled look. "Why not? What good is nice jewelry if you don't wear it? I'm sure your mother will say yes." She came back to the bed and sat cross-legged in front of me. "You're really acting weird today." Ivette pushed me back by the shoulders so that

I fell against the large pink pillows on my bed. "You need to let your hair down and relax. You're way too tense."

Doc Machado's silhouette and lifeless hands flashed before my eyes. I shook my head. I wanted to tell Ivette what I'd seen. I took a deep breath.

"Ivette?"

"Yes, *señorita*?" She was now practicing how to dance the cha-cha-cha with my teddy bear.

"Yesterday, I, um, I . . ."

She kept moving to the imaginary song in her head. "Go ahead, spit it out. I can dance and listen at the same time."

I couldn't say it. The words just wouldn't get out of my mouth.

"Nothing, never mind."

"You're just nervous about the dance. C'mon. Let's go to your mom's room and see what she's got that you can borrow." Ivette started walking toward the door.

I jumped up and pulled her toward the mirror. "Mamá doesn't keep her stuff there anymore. Look, what should I do with my hair?" I piled it on top of my head and let a few wisps fall around my shoulders.

Ivette stood behind me and looked into the mirror. "Nah, don't do that. Leave it down, but curl the ends. It'll look pretty with the dress's neckline. But you definitely need a nice necklace. Does your mom still have that gold chain with the tiny hearts hanging from it? That'd be perfect."

"I already told you, I can't."

"If your mom put it in the bank, then just ask your dad to pick it up tomorrow morning. He's got the keys to the place."

I lowered my voice. "It's not at the bank. Look, you have to promise not to tell, okay?"

Ivette nodded.

"Papá stashed away some of our stuff . . . for safekeeping. Just in case."

"In case of what?" Ivette twisted her mouth. "Isn't that exactly what Fidel says we shouldn't be doing? We're supposed to be open with the revolution. Let them know what we have, in case there's a better use for it."

"What's a better use for a necklace? My parents have worked hard for what they have, whether it's in the bank or in the floor."

"In the floor?"

I quickly shook my head. "*Nada*. Listen, your parents bought you a nice dress with money they've saved, and my parents are just saving up for whatever they want. It's basically the same thing, right?"

"I guess."

An uncomfortable silence filled the room. I glanced down at my hands and saw the ragged edges of my cuticles. I changed the subject back to fashion. "By the way, have you seen these things?" I lifted up both hands. "I was going to wear white gloves, but I think I should have a nice manicure underneath."

Ivette immediately perked up. "But of course! Those nails have to look nice. You need to have them pretty for when Manuel holds your hand." She smiled and everything seemed to get back on track.

I let out a nervous laugh. It was crazy how just mentioning Manuel got me all jittery, as if butterflies were fluttering around inside of me.

"I brought a couple of polishes from my house. Which one do you like?" Ivette grabbed her purse from the chair next to the window. "Looks like your dad and uncle are home." Ivette pointed down to the front yard.

I joined her by the window and saw Tío Antonio and Papá talking. I cranked the window open to shout hello, but the sudden harshness of their voices stopped me.

"*¡Basta!*" Papá threw his hands up in the air. "I've had enough! Papá would be rolling in his grave if he could hear you."

"Don't bring in our parents. They were from another era."

"Antonio, do what you want, but don't come crying to me when you and your *compañeros* get run out! You are on your own!"

Tío glared at Papá. "Fernando, you're going to regret this. Soon it'll be you who comes begging to *me*!"

He spun around and headed toward his brown convertible.

I quickly closed the window. Papá was not one to make a scene in public.

"Sorry," I muttered.

"Don't worry, brothers always fight. You should see my family when all my aunts, uncles, and cousins come over. We can get pretty loud, too. You're just not used to it because you've got a small family." Ivette put her hand on my shoulder. "He'll probably be back tomorrow, ready to eat one of your mom's famous *flans*."

I nodded, but all of my Manuel-induced butterflies had flown away, leaving me with a sick, empty feeling. I'd seen Papá and Tío argue before, but this time was different. And no matter what Ivette said, she knew it, too.

Chapter 9

THOUSANDS REMAIN IN CUBAN PRISONS
—*DAILY CHRONICLE*, MAY 27, 1961

"You look"—Frankie wiped his runny nose on his pajama sleeve—"nice. Kinda pretty."

"*Gracias,*" I said in a sing-song voice, and glided past the sofa. I twirled around, and the full skirt of my pink and white dress floated around me. It reminded me of something Sandra Dee would wear in one of the beach movies I'd seen. The top was sleeveless and cinched at the waist, and it was cut to give the illusion that I had curves in just the right places. Wearing Mamá's pink heels, I felt so grown-up. With two fingers, I picked up my small white gloves and placed them over the square patent-leather purse that sat on the dining room table. "Mamá, are you ready? It's almost eight."

Mamá's high heels clicked against the floor tiles as she came down the stairs. She wore a perfectly ironed, cream-colored linen dress, and her eyes sparkled with excitement, as if she were about to go to her first dance. "Put a little more powder on your nose, Lucía. You don't want it to get shiny by the end of the night," she said.

"I already put enough on. Can we just go?" All day long I had been imagining dancing with Manuel, holding his hand, maybe having him give me a good-night kiss.

"Not yet. Papá's not home and I can't leave Frankie by himself." She fumbled with the clasp on her bracelet. "Are you sure you don't want to wear your silver chain with the cross on it? It would look so pretty with that dress."

I giggled, remembering Ivette's performance with the chain. "No, it's okay." I walked over and checked the clock next to the sofa. Where was Papá?

"Does he know we're waiting for him?" I asked Mamá.

"Yes, yes. There was some sort of emergency at the bank. I already called, and Eduardo told me your father was in a meeting. That he'd be a little late." Mamá pointed a camera at me. "Stand still and smile, Lucía. I want to take a picture."

I posed and waited for the bulb to flash. Another picture for the family album.

A glance at the hallway clock reminded me that if I didn't get to the dance soon, Manuel might think I wasn't going at all. I opened the front door, hoping to see Papá's car pulling into the driveway. A soft breeze blew through my hair, and suddenly I realized that this would be the first time since Doc Machado's death that I'd gone outside. I shuddered, unsure if it was the cool breeze that made me shiver or the twinge of fear in my chest. Slow, deep breaths stifled the rising panic. I concentrated on the dance. On Manuel.

As I paced up and down the driveway, a brown convertible parked down the street caught my eye. It was Tío Antonio. Ivette had been right. He was probably here to apologize and make up with Papá. Maybe he could take me to the dance, and then Mamá could stay home with Frankie. That would be even better. I rushed over.

"Tío, what are you doing here?"

He flicked his cigarette out the open window. "I'm just waiting for your father."

"Oh. Can you talk to him later? I really need to ask you for a favor."

Tío raised an eyebrow.

"Remember how when I was little you'd let me stand on your shoes and you'd dance with me?"

He smiled. "*Sí,* I remember those days."

"Well, tonight is my first real dance."

"You need another lesson?" He reached into his pocket and pulled out a silver cigarette box.

"No, but Frankie's sick, Papá's stuck at the office, and Mamá can't leave to chaperone me. So I thought maybe . . ."

Tío Antonio tapped a cigarette against the steering wheel before lighting it. "So, *mi sobrina* wants her good old uncle to do the chaperoning. And you think your mother will agree to this?"

"Yes, yes." I bounced up and down. "I'll take care of it. Please, will you do it?"

He blew out a puff of smoke and nodded.

I threw my arms around his neck. "Thank you, Tío. You're the best!" I raced back toward the house.

Mamá stood in the doorway with her arms crossed. "*¿Qué quiere Antonio?* Is he here to argue again?"

"No, he's just waiting for Papá." I saw Mamá's eyes narrow. "He wants to apologize. He wants to straighten everything out."

Mamá dropped her arms and her face softened. "I knew he'd come to his senses. Family is family, after all." She looked over at the brown convertible. "Tell him to come inside. We can wait together until Papá gets home."

I looked back at my uncle casually smoking his cigarette. "Mamá, Tío says he can take me to the dance and be my chaperone. That way I won't be late and you can stay with Frankie."

Mamá waved her hands. "No, no. I think it's more appropriate if I chaperone you. It's your first dance."

"But if we keep waiting, I'll miss my first dance. Please. You can meet us there after Papá gets home. Just don't make me be late. Not tonight, please." I glanced back at Tío and waved.

"*Bueno*, I don't want you to be late." She thought it over. "Fine, but I'll take a taxi over there the moment your father gets home. Then your *tío* can come over and talk to your father in private." She nodded, approving of the idea. "Yes, a little time together alone is just what those two brothers need."

"Thank you, Mamá!" I turned around, held up a finger to let Tío Antonio know that I'd be back in a minute, then rushed into the house to get my purse and gloves.

Mamá trailed after me. "Lucía, wait, one more thing."

I quickly stopped to check my reflection in the hall mirror. My pink dress was still crisp, no sign of wrinkles anywhere. My hair still held a few curls at the bottom and there was no shine on my nose. Perfect.

"You do look beautiful, *mi hija*." Mamá beamed.

I turned and smiled. This night was going to be one I'd always remember.

"Here. I want you to wear these." Mamá reached for her diamond earrings and unscrewed the backs.

"Mamá, you never take those off."

"Tonight they're yours." She placed them in the palm of my hand. "Now go. Your *tío* is waiting. I'll be there in a little while." She gave me a quick kiss on the cheek.

❊   ❊   ❊   ❊   ❊

"I promise you won't have to stay long, Tío." I held my hair in one hand so that it wouldn't fly all over the place in the open convertible.

"Not a problem, Lucy." He adjusted the rearview mirror. "You can always count on me, even if I'm not your father's favorite person."

"Why are you in a fight with him?" I asked.

Tío Antonio shrugged. *"La vida."*

"Life?"

"Just the way life is. Fernando and I have always seen things differently. This time, though, he'll come around. He just needs to learn a few hard lessons." Tío Antonio took another drag from his cigarette.

I leaned back against the white leather seat. We were approaching the center of town. The park was nearby. I knew Doc Machado had already been buried, but I didn't want to see the tree or even the park entrance. I turned to face Tío Antonio.

"What's *patria potestad?*" I asked, partly because it bothered me that my parents had never answered my question, partly because I wanted an excuse not to think about Doc Machado.

"Wow, where'd you hear about that? No, wait, let me guess." Tío Antonio shook his head. *"Mi hermano."*

I sat, silently waiting.

"Patria potestad, huh? Okay, well, I think it's Latin. It means parents have the right to make decisions for their own kids." Tío brought the cigarette back up to his lips, this time leaving it dangling from the corner of his mouth. "But that's not why you heard about it." He glanced over at me. "Some people have this crazy idea

that Castro wants kids to be the property of the state." He then gave me a little smile and wink. "Like Fidel really wants to deal with thousands of pipsqueaks. Figure out where they should live and go to school." Tío shook his head. "The whole idea is silly."

"Yeah, I guess it does sound crazy."

The convertible turned sharply and I slid toward the passenger door. Tío chuckled. "Careful there, Slick." He pulled into a parking space in front of what used to be the very exclusive yacht club. *Un nido de parásitos,* a nest of parasites. That's what the newspapers had called the place before the revolution shut it down and turned it into a public meeting hall and cultural center.

Tío turned to face me. "Okay, I don't want to sit with all the mother hens inside. You'll be fine if I stay out here and smoke a few, right?"

I nodded, knowing that this was not going to go over well with Mamá.

"I'll be here if you need me. Ready for your big night?"

"Ready," I answered.

Chapter 10

CASTRO'S DEAL—PEOPLE FOR TRACTORS
—*THE WASHINGTON POST*, MAY 27, 1961

"*Chica,* you look gorgeous!" Ivette gave me a quick hug.

"You too," I said.

"Oh, this old thing?" Ivette gave me a wink and spun around in her new dress. If anyone else had worn it, they might've looked like one big domino, but Ivette made it work. She was a fashion queen.

I scanned the dance floor. There, under a canopy of white crepe-paper ribbons, ten couples danced as the band played a quick merengue. Next to them, along the back wall, sat the chaperones . . . all keeping a watchful eye on the dancing. I felt like Cinderella at the ball.

"He's over there," Ivette whispered, and pointed to a corner where some potted plants had been decorated with clear twinkling lights.

"Who?" I asked casually.

"Por favor." Ivette rolled her eyes.

Then I saw him. Manuel. Walking straight toward us in his light-colored suit and thin black tie. He looked like a movie star . . . Elvis, only better.

I swallowed the lump in my throat.

"Hi, Manuel. Did you see who just got here?" Ivette asked.

He nodded, scanning me from head to toe. *"Hola, Lucía,"* he said.

A slow Beny Moré song started to play.

"Hola." I looked down at the floor.

"I think my brother's looking for me." Ivette gave me a little nudge. "I'll catch you later."

I stood frozen. Not knowing what to say.

"Would you like to dance?" Manuel asked.

I took a deep breath and nodded.

Manuel took me by the hand and led me to the dance floor. In his arms, it felt like no one else mattered. I floated around the room.

The next song played was "The Twist," so we let go of each other but continued dancing together. I started to relax.

"Nice not to have to worry about school for a while, huh?" Manuel asked while Chubby Checker's song told us all to "come on and twist."

I nodded. "Señora Cardoza was never much fun."

Manuel laughed and rolled his eyes. Those beautiful green eyes. "Tell me about it. This is the second year

I have to take her class!" He pointed to the side of the dance floor. "You want to get a drink?"

"Okay," I answered, seeing Ivette and a few others by the punch bowl.

Manuel reached over and took my hand.

It was all I could do not to jump up and down. I felt a sudden urge to giggle . . . but somehow I faked being calm.

Ivette raised a single eyebrow as we walked over.

"So, I see you're having a good time," Raúl, Ivette's older brother, snickered.

"You bet," Manuel answered, dropping my hand to get our drinks.

I'd never hated cups so much in my life.

"Ready for our adventure, Raúl?" Manuel asked.

"You kidding? Absolutely. This is going to be the best summer of our lives. Out there, helping the revolution, what could be better?" Raúl took a sip of the punch.

"Maybe we'll catch some anti-revolutionaries on the way. Break up one of their plots. Show Fidel and Che that we're true soldiers!" Manuel said.

I thought of Doc Machado wanting to form a peaceful protest. How he'd been killed for that.

"I thought the brigades were only about teaching the peasants how to read. Part of the literacy campaign," I said.

"Sure, but we all have a duty to the revolution. Getting rid of *gusanos* is part of it. Look at Che. Fidel

put him in charge of the prisons, and he got rid of everyone who's against the revolution. He is one tough *hombre* . . . just like me," Manuel answered.

"You don't really mean that anyone who doesn't support Fidel should be killed, right?" The image of Doc
Machado, hanging, flashed before my eyes.

Manuel looked at me and then back at Raúl. "Well,
no, I mean only if they deserve it."

Somehow, Manuel didn't look like a movie star anymore. He started looking more and more like all the
other *brigadistas*.

He leaned over and whispered into my ear, "*Tranquila*, you've just got to say what they want to hear."

I pulled back and looked into his eyes. Maybe it was
the same thing my family was now doing. Playing the
game.

I smiled and nodded, understanding what he meant.

"So, you ready for Monday, Ivette?" Manuel asked.

Ivette almost spit up the punch she was drinking.
She started to cough.

I looked back at Manuel. "What else is happening on
Monday?"

"Didn't she tell you?" Raúl patted his sister on the
back. "She joined our brigade troop. We're all shipping
out together. First we go to Varadero for some extra
training, then we get our assignments."

I stared at Ivette, who had started to regain her com-
posure. "*¿Qué?* You joined the brigades?"

"I — I," Ivette stammered.

"And you didn't tell me? You're leaving in two days and you didn't even tell me!"

"I didn't even know until a couple of days ago. I wasn't planning on leaving so soon, but Mother thought it was best if I went with Raúl." Ivette rolled her eyes. "She says it's my duty. I was going to tell you yesterday, but I didn't know how. Then my mother told me what you'd seen in the park and that you were upset. I thought I'd just tell you after the dance. I didn't want to make you feel worse." She reached for my arm.

I yanked it away. "I can't believe you. Keeping something this big from me. I thought you were my best friend."

"I am."

I looked around. "I need to get some air."

Manuel took my hand. "C'mon. We'll go outside."

I followed him out a side door, happy to leave Ivette and her lies behind me. The crisp night air felt good as it filled my lungs. Slowly it doused my anger.

"Don't blame Ivette. It's hard to say good-bye, even if it's only for a few months." Manuel led me to a bench near the golf course.

We sat down.

"She never seemed to be into the revolution. I feel like I don't even know her. And when did she join? She could've told me then, right?"

Manuel smiled. "You know you really look very

beautiful tonight, Lucía." He pushed a strand of hair away from my face.

Suddenly I realized that I was outside, on a beautiful clear night, with a million stars twinkling above me, sitting on a bench next to Manuel. *The* Manuel. My heart started pounding so hard that I was afraid Manuel might be able to hear it.

Slowly he leaned over and put his lips on mine. I felt the electricity run up and down my spine.

Who cared about Ivette? I had just had my first kiss . . . and it was perfect!

After a moment, I pulled back and smiled.

"We should go back in. People will wonder where we are," I whispered.

Manuel inched closer to me. "Why? Your mother isn't even here yet." He kissed me again, but harder this time.

I turned my head. "Manuel, I don't—"

"Shhh." He pushed me against the edge of the bench's arm. "Don't you want me to remember you while I'm gone?"

"Yes, but . . . ," I whispered.

The look in Manuel's eyes told me he wasn't listening. He licked his lips and leaned over me.

"Manuel." I tried to get out from under him. "Please don't."

He laughed and tightened his grip. He straddled me to keep me from moving. One of his hands slipped down my neck toward my chest. As he tried to kiss me again,

I twisted away, my knee accidentally catching him squarely between the legs.

"Uh!" Manuel grunted as he fell to the ground. He glared up at me. "You stupid *gusana*. You're a worm just like your father!"

I jumped off the bench and ran toward the front of the building, tears building up in my eyes.

I quickly spotted Tío leaning against his convertible, talking to a soldier. I wiped my eyes and calmly walked toward them.

"Tío, I want to go home," I said, a little out of breath.

He looked at his watch. "Now? It's still early. Go back in and have some fun." He turned his attention back to the soldier.

I grabbed his arm. "No, Tío. I want to leave now."

He gave me a stern look. "Lucía, I brought you all the way out here. Now I'm having an important conversation with Capitán García. We'll leave in a little while."

I turned around, not knowing where to go. I couldn't go back to the party and face Manuel, and I was too afraid to walk home by myself. I'd have to hide in the bathroom. I rushed into the building and ran toward the bathroom door.

"Lucy!" Ivette chased after me.

I grabbed the handle and hurried inside.

"Lucía, please." Ivette followed me in. She pulled me by the elbow, spinning me around. "You're crying! What's wrong? What happened?"

I shook my head. Everything had gone wrong. I'd acted like a little girl in front of Manuel, and now I was humiliated.

Ivette peered into my eyes. "I'm sorry for not telling you about the brigades. I should've. Talk to me."

I balled up some toilet paper and wiped my eyes. "I'm sorry, too." I looked at myself in the mirror. All dressed up, pretending to be grown-up, and inside I couldn't even handle a kiss. In between blowing my nose and splashing water on my face, I told Ivette everything that had happened, play-by-play. When I was done, I expected her to tell me that next time I'd be more prepared, that I wouldn't get so scared by a boy trying to make out with me.

"*¿Qué se cree él?* Does he really think he's all that? I'm going to give him a piece of my mind!" Anger blazed across Ivette's eyes.

"No," I said, looking down.

"You sure? I can really make his life miserable . . . somehow."

I shook my head. She was truly my best friend. "I just want to go home, but Tío won't leave."

"Okay, stay here." Ivette yanked open the door. "I'll find my mom and tell her we both feel sick. That we must've eaten bad shrimp or something."

I nodded and leaned against the bathroom sink. How could this night get any worse?

Chapter 11

THE RED PLOT CONFIRMED
—*CHICAGO DAILY TRIBUNE*, MAY 27, 1961

On the drive home, I kept my eyes closed. Ivette's mom probably thought I really was sick, but all I was doing was replaying the entire scene with Manuel over and over again. The way we'd danced and held hands. How he changed when we were alone. The scorn in his face when he called me a *gusana*. How could someone seem so perfect and then rip out your heart?

"*¡Ay! ¿Qué habrá pasado?*" Ivette's mother exclaimed as she pulled the car into the driveway.

I opened my eyes to see two police and military vehicles parked in front of my house. Thoughts of Señor Betafil and Doc Machado filled my head.

I jumped out of the car and ran to the front door, Ivette and her mother only steps behind me. "Papá! Mamá!" I shouted.

A soldier opened the door.

"*¡Mi hija!* We're here!" Mamá called out.

Inside, soldiers were making a mess of the house. There were drawers emptied out onto the tables. Furniture was moved. The loose tile on the floor was lifted up.

Papá sat at the dining room table with his hands cuffed behind him.

"*Ven acá,* Lucía. Stay with me." Mamá sat on the sofa holding Frankie, his eyes wide with fear.

A policeman stood over them. Hands on his rifle.

I rushed over and sat next to Mamá.

"*¿Por qué . . . ?*" I tried to absorb everything. "Why are they here?"

Mamá opened her mouth to speak, but Ivette and her mother walked into the room.

"Sonia, *¿qué pasó?* What did you do?" Ivette's mother asked.

"*We* did nothing," Mamá answered.

The officer chuckled. "Nothing, eh? Illegally withdrawing items from the bank, hoarding cash and jewelry. Probably working with the underground." He looked over at Ivette's mother. "That sound like nothing to you, Marcela?"

"I tried to warn them." She pulled Ivette toward her. "You see. This is what I've been telling you. You can't trust people like this."

"People like this?" Mamá stood up. There was fire in her eyes. "You mean good people who you've known your whole life. People who don't follow every little thing Fidel says. Who actually have minds and question what is happening?"

Ivette's mother threw up her hands. "*Vámonos,* Ivette. There's no getting through to them. They're just like the Yankee *imperialistas.*"

Ivette stood frozen by the doorway as her mother walked out. She stared at me and then at the hole in the floor. I couldn't tell if her gaze was one of pity, fear, or guilt. She slowly turned to leave.

Mamá smoothed back her hair and sat down. "How could anyone have known about the jewelry?" she muttered. "No one knew. We never said a word . . . to anyone."

I looked over at Ivette walking out. She knew. She'd heard me say it was in the floor.

I stood up. "I need to talk to Ivette. Can I go outside a moment?"

The police officer motioned for me to go ahead, but I wasn't talking to him. I looked at Mamá and she nodded. Guilt washed over me as I realized that this was all my fault. If only I hadn't trusted my best friend.

I hurried outside and grabbed Ivette by the shoulder before she stepped off the porch.

"Lucy, I'm so—"

"Save it!" I said in a low voice. "I know it was you! How could you? I thought you were my friend!"

"What? You don't think I—"

"You're the only one who knew. You lied about the *brigadistas*, about leaving. Did you think this would get you bonus points with your new *comrades*? I'm sure you and Manuel will have a big laugh about all of this!"

Ivette's mother honked the car horn, and Ivette motioned for her to wait just one more minute.

"Lucy, you're not serious. We're best friends—"

"You said it was wrong for us to hide our things."

"Yeah, but I'd never—"

"No one else knew." I shook my head. "Only you. And look what your mother thinks of us!"

"So, this is the thanks I get after defending you for weeks! Fine. I certainly don't need to stand here and be accused of something I didn't do! Go back to your traitor family. See if I care!" Ivette stormed off the porch and ran back to her mother's waiting car.

"I never want to see you again!" I shouted as the car pulled out of the driveway.

I turned and walked back into the chaos.

Papá was being told to stand up.

"Wait!" I ran toward him.

A soldier blocked me.

"*Tranquila,* Lucy. They just want to ask me some questions at the station. Everything'll be fine." Papá tried to smile.

But I'd heard stories of people being arrested and never coming back. Of the *paredón.* The firing squad.

"No! Please." Tears stung my eyes.

An officer grabbed me by the arms before I could move. I looked back at Mamá, frozen on the sofa holding Frankie, who had hidden his face in her chest. A soldier had his rifle aimed directly at them.

Papá marched right by me, his head held up high. Quietly he whispered, "I'll be fine. Take care of your mother."

Huge tears ran down my cheeks. The lump in my throat barely allowed me to breathe. I nodded as Papá was led out of our house.

Seconds passed, but it felt like years.

As the last of the soldiers walked out, one of them looked at our terrified faces and laughed. Before leaving, he turned and spat on the floor. "*¡Gusanos!*" he said.

The door slammed shut.

Mamá turned to look out the window. "Fernaaando!" she wailed, but he was already gone.

Chapter 12

A Blow to the Anti-Castro Cause
—*The Los Angeles Times*, May 29, 1961

"*Gracias,* Antonio. Anything you can do." Mamá wrapped the phone cord around her hand. "It's just that it's been over twenty-four hours and they haven't told us anything. We've been so worried."

I looked at Mamá's eyes. There seemed to be a sense of relief in them. I waited for her to finish.

"No, no. Don't worry. I won't say a word. I know he has his pride. Yes, I'll make sure to tell her. *Adiós.*" Mamá hung up and placed a hand over her heart.

"Well? What did he say?" I asked.

"Your uncle talked to some friends he has on the police force. He says Papá's fine. That they haven't officially charged him with anything yet." Mamá ran her fingers through her hair. "It'll all be fine. He'll be home soon."

"He will? When? Today?" Frankie ran down the stairs.

"I'm not sure, *mi hijo*. But soon. And Lucía, Antonio also apologized for not bringing you home from the dance. Said he didn't know that you weren't feeling well." Mamá gave me a small smile. "You must've given him quite a scare when he realized you were gone." She looked down as she went to twist her wedding ring and realized it wasn't there. "I keep forgetting." She shook her head.

"I'm sorry they took it," I said.

Mamá put an arm around me. "Nothing for you to be sorry about. It's not your fault. Antonio even thinks they might return it. Although whatever we had hidden away they'll probably keep . . . just to prove a point."

I looked down. It was my fault. I'd confided in Ivette. Even letting it slip that Papá had hidden things in the floor. Guilt ate me up inside. But how could I tell my parents that this was all because of me?

Mamá tugged at her ear and touched her diamond stud earring. "Look. Thanks to you, I still have these."

They were the only valuables the soldiers didn't take. I was glad she'd let me wear them to the dance.

"I'm gonna check the mail," Frankie announced.

Mamá nodded and picked up a broom that lay against the wall. She started sweeping the foyer and porch.

"Maybe you should take the earrings off," I said. "What if someone sees you?"

She shrugged. "Doesn't matter. If the government wants to take them, they will. But for now, I'll wear them. Your father will love to see that I have them on."

"Hey, Lucy, there's a note for you," Frankie said coming back inside.

"For me?"

"Yeah, it's from Ivette."

"I don't want it. Throw it away."

Mamá stopped sweeping. "Lucía, I know you're upset. But Ivette's been a good friend to you. She called three times yesterday. We can't blame her for what her mother thinks."

I could certainly blame her. And if Mamá knew what she'd done, then she'd understand why I was never going to talk to her again.

"She told me yesterday that she was leaving today with the brigades," Mamá said.

"Mmm-hmm."

"You know that can't be her idea. It has to be her parents'. I'm sure fashion is not a priority for the *brigadistas*."

"So?"

"Don't you want to talk to her before she leaves? She's probably nervous, and it may be a while before you can see her again."

"Fine." I snatched the note from Frankie's hand. "Let me see what she says."

"You don't have to be so rude!" Frankie shouted as I ran up the stairs.

In the quiet of my room, I opened the envelope and read the letter.

> Dear Lucy,
>
> I'm sorry for everything that happened to your family. I know you think I had something to do with it, but I promise that I didn't. I'm leaving for Varadero with the brigades in a few hours and I was hoping to talk to you. If you get this message in time, please call me.
>
> Your friend,
> Ivette

I put the note on the bed. Maybe Ivette hadn't betrayed us. Maybe she was telling the truth. But then how did the soldiers know to look under the tiles? I paced around the room. Frankie had been sick in bed the whole time, so he couldn't have told anyone. Mamá and Papá hadn't said anything, either. Who else could it be?

The front door creaked as it closed. I grabbed the paper and walked downstairs. Mamá and Frankie had gone outside, and the black hallway phone seemed to wait for my decision.

If I could slip up and tell Ivette about Papá hiding the valuables, maybe she'd accidentally told someone. She always loved to gossip. But then why not just admit it? Or at least give us a warning so we could move the stuff?

Frankie's voice filtered into the room through the open window. "Can't we see Papá even if he's in jail?" he asked Mamá.

I looked at Ivette's note one more time. My decision was made. I crumpled up the paper and threw my friendship away.

Chapter 13

"He'll be here any minute." Mamá plumped up the small pillow resting on Papá's favorite chair.

I peered out the large picture window. The last four days had seemed to last a lifetime, but these final moments were the longest. Then a familiar silhouette walked down the sidewalk. "I see him!" I shouted.

Papá's slow stride hinted at exhaustion, but there was still a sense of pride in how he carried himself.

"*¡Gracias, Dios mío!*" Mamá made the sign of the cross and checked her lipstick in the hall mirror.

Frankie ran and opened the door. "Papá!"

Papá smiled and hurried up the walkway. We met him halfway and smothered him with hugs and kisses.

"Let's get inside," he said. The four of us moved together, as a unit, no one wanting to let go.

Once inside, we all walked over to Papá's chair and helped him sit down. His clothes were dirty and rumpled. He smelled like the amphitheater bathrooms after a big concert, but I couldn't get enough of him. To me, he had never looked so good.

"So, they dropped all the charges, right, Fernando?" Mamá asked.

Papá nodded. "Most of them. But they're keeping everything we hid away."

"I don't care about any of that." Mamá reached for his hand and put it against her cheek. "I'm just so glad to have you home." She gave the palm of his hand a kiss.

Frankie leapt onto Papá's lap. "So, the soldiers won't be back, right, Papá?"

"Frankie! Papá's tired. Get off him." I grabbed Frankie by the arm.

"No, it's all right, Lucy. Here, sit next to me, too." Papá scooted over in the chair so I could squeeze in next to him. "And no, Frankie, I don't expect the soldiers to come back. But things are going to change for us." He sighed and looked at Mamá sitting by his feet. "Here, first let me give you this." He reached into his pocket and pulled out Mamá's wedding ring.

"Fernando, you got it back!"

Papá smiled and nodded. Mamá immediately slipped it onto her finger.

"But that's about all I have." He looked down. "I lost my job at the bank."

"*Ay,* Fernando." Mamá covered his large hands with her small ones.

Papá shook his head. "No, it was expected. It was just a matter of time."

"You'll get an even better job, Papá," I said, trying to be positive.

"It'll be difficult, Lucy." He stroked my hair. "The government controls all the industries. We're going to have to make some adjustments."

"Fernando, I can work." Mamá started to get up. "Take in some sewing. Maybe a little ironing."

"No, no. I won't have my wife working. I'll find something. Try to get some work as a handyman. See how that goes."

"But, Papá, can't you convince them to give you another job . . . in an office?" I thought about how I'd never seen Papá fix anything around our house.

"No, *mi hija.* I've been told that I need to prove myself first."

"Prove yourself how?" Mamá tucked in her cotton blouse.

He shrugged. "Show them I'm a good revolutionary." He looked at me and Frankie. "They mentioned the kids several times. Said that Lucía needs to volunteer to work on the farms or join the brigades if she wants to finish her education. And Frankie'll have to join the Pioneros group to learn all about the revolution."

"No." Mamá put her hands on her hips. "I won't do that. There's no way I'm sending my daughter away. Revolutionaries taking care of her. It's absurd!"

Papá nodded. "I know, I know. They want to indoctrinate the kids right under our noses."

"There's got to be another way. I'll study from home," I said.

"Me too. It'll be fun!" Frankie smiled.

I shot Frankie a nasty look. "This isn't about fun." I turned to Mamá. "Maybe they'll excuse us from the service. Tío Antonio can ask about getting us some type of special permission."

"Don't mention your *tío's* name again!" Papá abruptly stood up, nearly dropping Frankie to the ground. "We don't have anything to do with him!"

"Fernando, he's your brother. He made calls to try to get you out of jail. I know you fought the other day, but—"

"Ha!" Papá threw his head back and laughed. "He told you he was trying to get me out, eh?" Papá shook his head. "*¡Qué maldito!* He saw me in jail this morning and you know what he did?"

None of us said a word.

"He told me that I'd asked for all of this. That it was my fault. Said he'd warned me, but that now I deserved whatever came my way!"

Mamá shook her head. *"Pero —"*

Papá interrupted. "But nothing! From now on, we have to expect the worst and hope for the best." He looked at all three of us. "We can't count on anyone, anymore."

Not even best friends, I thought.

Chapter 14

FIDEL SENDS TOTS TO REDS
—*THE DELAWARE COUNTY DAILY TIMES*, JUNE 2, 1961

It had been two days since Papá came home and four since Ivette left with the brigades. In under a week, my whole world had changed.

"Can't we go for a little while?" Frankie held his beach towel in one hand and his fishing pole in the other. "It's summer."

Mamá shook her head. "I already said no, Frankie."

Frankie gave Mamá his sad-puppy face. "What if Papá takes me?"

"He's not even home right now." Mamá pulled back the kitchen curtain and looked out the window.

"Please, Mamá, Lucía can take me. You'll go, right, Lucy?" He glanced over at me as I finished my lunch.

I shook my head. The last thing I wanted to do was run into soldiers, *brigadistas,* or anyone from school.

After what happened at the dance and Papá's arrest, I wasn't sure how I'd be treated.

"Frankie, *por favor*, give it a rest." Mamá opened the back door just an inch and looked outside. Frankie stomped out of the room.

"What are you looking at?" I asked, noticing my mother's odd behavior.

"*Nada.*" She closed the door. "I'm just waiting for Alicia Milian. She's supposed to stop by."

"Laura's mother?"

Mamá picked up my empty plate and took it to the sink. "Mmm-hmm."

"I didn't know you were friends."

"Hmm." She snuck another look out the window. "Not really friends."

"Is Laura coming over, then?" I gulped down the last of my lemonade.

Mamá looked at me as if she'd just noticed I was talking. "*¿Qué dijiste?* You asked about Laura?"

"Mamá, what's going on?"

"*Nada*, I said. But why don't you go upstairs with your brother. Laura's not coming and her mother's only dropping something off for me." She began to dry some of the dishes.

"Everything okay?" I asked, remembering how much she and Papá had argued the night before. They'd thought I was asleep, but I could hear their muffled voices going back and forth until well past midnight.

"*Sí,* everything's fine." Mamá dried her hands and pulled back the curtain. "She's here." She took off her apron and straightened her blouse. "Now go!"

❋ ❋ ❋ ❋ ❋

That night, Papá called Frankie and me into the living room. He was pacing back and forth. Something was terribly wrong.

"*Mi hija,* sit down." He gestured over to the sofa. "Please."

"What's going on?" I looked over at my mother, sitting in the armchair, hands crossed on her lap. A vacant look in her eyes.

Frankie came into the room bouncing a ball. "*¿Qué,* Papá?"

"Come here, Frankie." Papá tousled Frankie's hair, then took the ball and placed it on the floor next to the table. "Sit over there, next to your sister."

Papá's somber mood frightened me. "Did something happen?"

"No, but after . . ."

My heart thumped loudly in my ears. "Are they going to arrest you again?" I asked.

"No," he said.

"Does it have something to do with that man who came by a little while ago?" I thought about the short man wearing a hat who'd stayed in the shadows of our front porch talking to Papá.

"Please, Lucy, don't interrupt. This is hard enough." Papá looked away.

Silence filled the room.

He took a deep breath and knelt down in front of Frankie and me. He reached for our hands.

"*Hijos*, you've both heard us talking about how the government wants you to be more active in the revolution."

Frankie and I nodded at the same time.

"Your mother and I don't want that for you. We fear that it'll change you. You'll begin to accept what they tell you as the truth. We don't want to lose you to something like that."

"You won't lose us," I said softly.

Papá smiled and looked over at Mamá. She stared at the floor.

"You think that now. But Frankie's young. He won't even realize it." Papá touched my cheek. I noticed a slight tremble in his hand. "And you, *mi hija preciosa*. They won't even let you finish school if you don't join the revolution."

He stood, put his hands in his pockets, and took a few steps back.

"This is so hard," he muttered.

"Papá . . ." I leaned forward, afraid that I already knew what he was about to say.

"Your mother and I have decided . . ." Papá walked

over and put his arm on Mamá's shoulder. She sat frozen in place. "We've made plans for you to leave Cuba . . . tomorrow."

My heart stopped.

"You and Mamá, too, right?" Frankie asked.

My head spun. Leave Cuba? Tomorrow?

"No, Frankie, your mother and I . . ."

"They're not going with us." My fear turned into anger. "You're sending us away, aren't you? Like some of the other kids. How can you do that?"

Papá's eyes glistened. "Lucy, we have no choice. You know they won't let us leave with you. Alicia Milian was able to get us some visa waivers for you and Frankie, but . . ."

"Wait. So where are we going?" Frankie asked.

"To the U.S.," Papá answered. "It won't be for long, but you'll be safe until things get better here."

I jumped up. "No! You didn't even ask us! I won't be shipped off!"

Frankie slowly realized what was about to happen. "We don't know anyone there. I can't speak English." He turned around. "Mamá!"

Mamá kept her eyes focused on the floor.

"No! I won't do it and you can't make me!" Frankie darted out of the room.

I wanted to do the same. Scream, yell, beg, whatever it took.

Papá turned to me. "Lucy, please understand. It's the

only way to protect you." He placed his hand on my back, but I pulled away. "*Mi hija,* you're old enough to know that it's our only real choice. These brigades are only the beginning. Hundreds of children have already been sent to Russia and Czechoslovakia on supposed scholarships. And it won't end there."

"But, Papá . . ."

He shook his head. "Soon *all* kids will be forced to leave their families to go work in the fields cutting sugar cane, and then they'll be sent away to government schools. We won't have any say as to what happens to you or Frankie."

"But if you send us to the U.S., we still won't be together."

"True, but I'd rather have you safe, living with a good family in the U.S., than staying in your own country with these godforsaken soldiers."

The slow realization that nothing I said or did could change his mind washed over me.

"I'm so sorry, Lucy. It *has* to be this way." Papá walked over and stood by Mamá, who had not yet looked up.

My head seemed to nod on its own, without any instruction from me.

"All right, I guess you should go up and pack. We're leaving for the airport in Havana first thing tomorrow."

I walked toward the stairs, numb.

"Lucy," he called out, "you're only allowed to take

one bag, and a box of cigars that you can sell once you get there, so pack a little of everything, but nothing of value. The soldiers will steal it if they think it's worth something." Papá placed his arm around Mamá. "And, *mi hija*, thank you for not making this any harder."

As I left the room, I saw Mamá's shoulders shake and tears stream down her cheeks. Papá reached into his back pocket and pulled out a handkerchief. He offered it to her while his own tears fell to the floor.

Chapter 15

CUBAN REFUGEES SET FOR LONG EXILE—
FLIGHTS BOOKED SOLID
—*THE CHRISTIAN SCIENCE MONITOR*, JUNE 3, 1961

"Remember to use your manners. Say please and thank you." Mamá spoke quickly as we walked to the boarding area. "Don't forget that they are helping us."

I watched as passengers, both adults and children, formed a line by a glass partition. We had approached the *pecera*. The fish bowl. It was a nickname given to the waiting room because of the large glass walls that separated it from the rest of the airport. A soldier with a rifle slung over his back stood at the entrance. No one, except passengers with tickets, was allowed to enter. A little girl ran back from the line to clutch her mother again. Her father chased after her and tried to pull her away. Families all around us were saying their final good-byes.

"We love you both with all our hearts." Papá bent down and gave Frankie a hug and a kiss. "We'll send for you soon." He leaned over and whispered in my ear, "Things will get better and then you'll come back. Maybe by the end of summer. Until then, you have to be strong and take care of Frankie." He wrapped his arms around me. "I love you, *preciosa*."

Frankie and I threw our arms around Papá. "We love you, too." I choked back the tears.

"Now, what did I say? No more crying." Papá pulled away. "We've all done enough of that, and this is only temporary." He crouched down to look Frankie in the eye. "Remember, the Catholic Church in Miami is helping us, but if someone asks who's meeting you, tell them you're waiting for George."

Frankie nodded. "But who's George?"

Papá shook his head. "I'm not sure, but that's what you're supposed to say. It's a code."

"Like the spy movies, right?" I asked.

"Yes," he said, smiling, "just like in the movies." He gave us another hug, then picked up our small suitcases and carried them as far as the soldier standing guard would allow.

I faced Mamá. Her tears flowed freely.

"Frankie, *pórtate bien*. Behave and listen to your sister." She hugged him and then straightened his jacket. Mamá had told us to wear our best clothing so we'd make a good impression. Frankie had on a suit he'd worn once to a cousin's wedding, and I'd chosen a yellow dress with embroidered flowers on the edges. "You know I love you with all that I am." She gave him a big kiss on the cheek and hugged him again.

"Sonia, the flight . . . ," Papá called out from a few feet away. "Frankie, *vamos.*"

"No!" Frankie clutched Mamá. "I don't want to go!"

Papá walked over and pried Frankie away. As they stepped toward the line of passengers, Frankie kept glancing back at Mamá.

I watched my mother and studied her face. I wanted to memorize everything about her. The feel of her skin, the scent of her perfume. Her eyes, her smile, her hair. Then I noticed something was missing.

"Mamá, your earrings!"

Her hand touched a bare ear. "I know, *mi hija.*" She smiled. "Small price to pay to get airline tickets for you and Frankie."

"But they were Abuela's."

"And you are mine." She put her arms around me. "I love you, Lucía. More than you can imagine."

I began to cry. "I love you, too."

"Now, you need to go." She turned me around and nudged me toward the entrance of the *pecera*. "Don't worry, I'll be right here until your plane leaves."

❀   ❀   ❀   ❀   ❀

The bearded soldier ruffled through my nicely folded clothes and checked all of the suitcase's pockets.

Finding nothing of value, he slammed the bag closed and waved us through.

I spotted two empty chairs on the far side of the room. "C'mon, Frankie," I said, taking his hand.

"Whoa! Get back over here!" a woman in fatigues yelled at us.

I glanced back and noticed a line of children standing by a wall. Some were only four or five years old, others were teenagers.

"Are you traveling alone?" the woman asked as we walked toward her. "On visa waivers?"

I nodded.

"Then you have to wait here. We'll let you know when you can go."

Frankie and I obediently went to the back of the line. I expected to receive instructions on where we should sit on the plane or how we were supposed to claim our luggage when we arrived in Miami.

A few minutes later, two soldiers, a man and a woman, came out of a back room. Two teenage girls came out of the room in tears, followed by a boy about eleven years old. The young boy wasn't crying, or at least I couldn't tell if he was because he had his shoulders hunched over and seemed to be keeping his head down low.

"We are conducting random searches for contraband," announced the male soldier. "Compañera Pérez and I will be selecting a few of you to come with us to ensure that you are not trying to take Cuba's riches with you." He paused and looked at everyone from the first little girl in line to Frankie, who was at the end. "If you are hiding something in or under your clothing, I suggest you turn it over to us now. You *will* be asked to undress."

No one moved.

"Fine." He looked at the female guard. "Margarita, should it be every fourth or fifth child?"

My heart leapt to my throat. I started to tremble. Not that I feared they'd find something of value in my clothes, because they wouldn't. Papá had warned us over and over again about not trying to hide anything. It was the fear of what they'd do once we were naked and nothing was found.

Frankie stepped forward a little and puffed out his chest. "Don't worry, Lucy. I won't let them touch you," he whispered.

I smiled and gently pulled him back in line. There was nothing a seven-year-old could do to stop the search, but somehow I felt better knowing that his thoughts were on protecting me.

"*El quinto gusano,*" sneered the woman. Slowly every fifth child was pulled out of the line.

I held my breath as the female soldier curled her lip and pointed to me and Frankie, saying, "Three . . . four . . ." Frankie and I were not chosen. "The rest of you . . . take a seat. You'll be notified when the plane is ready to leave."

A sigh of relief escaped from my lips as the soldiers

herded three other kids into a small room. Immediately I felt guilty. One of the girls picked wasn't much older than Frankie. I looked over at the window separating us from the rest of the airport. I could see Mamá's tear-stained face next to the glass.

"I'm here," she mouthed.

I nodded.

"Let's sit, Lucy." Frankie led me through the crowded room to a couple of empty plastic chairs. We sat down next to an old man who fanned himself with his boarding ticket.

Frankie put his arm around me. My brother was so little, but he acted so big and tough. I leaned over and gave him a kiss on the cheek.

"Yuck!" He wiped his face. "Why'd you have to do that?"

I smiled.

"Lucía, I thought it was you!" a voice exclaimed.

I turned to see Laura Milian.

"I'm sorry to hear about your dad," she said.

The old man next to me moved over so Laura could sit down.

"How'd you know?" I imagined all the gossip going around town and how, at least, I wouldn't have to hear the whispers.

"My mom told me. She mentioned you might be leaving, too, but I had no idea we'd be on the same flight."

"Oh." I recalled how Mamá had acted while waiting

for Laura's mother to come by. It was only yesterday, but it already felt like weeks ago.

"It stinks when family betrays you. It happened to us, too. I think it was my mom's cousin who turned in my dad."

I raised my eyebrows. "What do you mean?"

Laura leaned over and lowered her voice. "You know, that your uncle turned you guys in . . . at least, that's what I heard. It's like when my father . . ."

I sat still, trying to absorb what Laura had just said. Could it be? No, it was just a nasty rumor. Tío Antonio didn't even know about the stuff being hidden. And Papá had argued with him, so he certainly didn't tell him about it. Unless that's what they were arguing about. But Papá would never have said anything to anyone . . . not even Tío. I wasn't even supposed to know. No, it was Ivette who'd betrayed us. But how could I clear Tío's name without admitting that I'd confided in Ivette in the first place?

"Ahem." Frankie tapped me on the shoulder. "Are you still in there, Lucy?"

I realized that Laura had stopped talking and they were both just staring at me.

"Uh, yeah." I faced Laura. "What makes you think it was my uncle?"

She shrugged. "My mom's cousin, Magda, the one who turned in my dad, came by to try to convince my mom to sign me up for the brigades . . . show people that we didn't agree with my father. Anyway, she mentioned how it was her duty to turn my dad in. Said others were doing it too . . . like your uncle."

"Tío wouldn't do that," Frankie said. "Would he?"

"Nah, it wasn't him," I answered. It was all secondhand gossip.

"Well, Magda was pretty convinced. She said he bragged about it at a CDR meeting. How he knew because your dad used to hide stuff under loose tiles when they were kids."

A sinking feeling started deep in my stomach. It hadn't been Ivette. She'd told me the truth . . . and now it was too late. She was gone and now I'd be leaving, too.

I looked over at my parents standing by the window. Someone had to tell them about Tío. About what he'd done.

"Stay here, Frankie," I ordered. "Don't move." I walked over to the glass partition.

"It was Tío who turned Papá in," I said in a low, quick voice.

Mamá shook her head. I could see her lips form the word *"qué."*

The noise in the room and the thickness of the glass wouldn't let us hear each other.

I looked at Papá. I wanted him to read my mind. Slowly I mouthed the words, "It . . . was . . . Tío."

Papá nodded. I could see the pain in his face. He stared at me and said, "I know."

An announcement was made. "Flight one ninety to Miami is now boarding."

Mamá tapped on the glass. "Look for me." She grabbed Papá's hand. "We'll be outside."

"How will I know where . . ." A crowd of people pressed against the window, pushing my parents out of the way. Everyone wanted a chance to say a final good-bye.

"Lucy!" Frankie's voice pierced the noise of all the passengers getting ready to board the plane.

"Coming!" I glanced back at the many tearful faces against the window. There were none that I recognized.

"Lucy!" Frankie shouted again.

I weaved through several people already gathered by the boarding gate. Frankie was sitting exactly where I left him.

"They're taking us into the plane first." Laura pointed to a pretty stewardess who stood with a group of children. "We need to go over there."

"Okay. Ready, Frankie?" I asked.

Frankie's silent tears gave me my answer.

❈　❈　❈　❈　❈

It was a bright, clear day outside. Not a cloud in the sky. I stared through the plane window at the palm trees in the distance. It didn't seem real. Like a painting was hung inside the plane showing us a glimpse of Cuba. I pushed my nose against the glass. Mamá and Papá were out there . . . somewhere.

"Can you see them?" Frankie unbuckled his seat belt and leaned over my shoulder.

"No."

A small crowd of people had gathered on the airport roof.

"Are they there?" he asked.

I shrugged. "I can't tell. It's too far away."

"But you told me that Mamá said to look for her."

"I know. I'm sure she's over there." A sadness washed over me. I wanted one last glimpse, one more connection with my parents.

The plane engines began to hum and we started to slowly roll forward.

"Look!" Frankie pointed to the rooftop.

There, in the middle of the small crowd, against the bright blue sky, a big red umbrella opened up. Mamá's umbrella.

That big stupid thing had never looked so beautiful. A smile edged its way onto my face. Mamá had found a way to say good-bye.

I didn't know when I'd be coming back home, so I studied everything about that moment. The trembling of the plane, the deafening sound of the engines as we lifted off the ground, the view of Havana's high-rises set against Cuba's rugged landscape, and the ever-shrinking red dot on top of the airport roof.

I caught my breath and simply whispered, *"Adiós."*

Chapter 16

ARRESTS INTENSIFIED IN CUBA PROVINCE
—*THE HARTFORD COURANT*, JUNE 3, 1961

"Flight crew, prepare for landing," the pilot announced.

The words pulled me out of my daze. I stared out the window as several large hotels came into view. Even from up high, they all seemed bigger than I'd imagined. It was like I had assumed that only Havana had tall buildings.

As the plane flew over the beach, the people down below looked like ants wandering in and out of the water. They seemed so carefree. I'd never been on a plane before, and seeing things from this altitude gave me a new perspective on how small we really were.

I closed my eyes and imagined Mamá and Papá were with us. I wished they could see all of this and that we were just here on a family vacation.

I opened my eyes to the sounds of a little girl sobbing

a few seats in front of me. It was no use pretending this was an ordinary trip. We weren't choosing to come here, and we had no idea when we'd be going back home.

It had been less than an hour since we'd left Cuba, and for the first time, I was entering a different country, a different world, a different life. I remembered Mamá's umbrella. It was no longer here to protect us, and neither was she.

Frankie leaned over my lap to get a better look out the window.

"Whoa, look at that building! It has to be at least a hundred stories high, don't you think?" Frankie pointed to the skyline.

"More like twenty . . . and we have buildings like that in Havana," I said.

From the air, the beach reminded me of Cuba with its coconut palms, turquoise water, and white sand, but as we went farther inland, the rest of Miami looked very different. Everything seemed to be set up in perfect lines and squares. And just past the tall buildings, everything was flat. There were no lush green mountains or rolling hills falling into the sea.

My stomach somersaulted as the plane dropped again. We were about to touch down and step into a country we didn't know. Would it really be like the movies I'd seen, with beautiful people everywhere, or would it be a place full of hate and race riots like the Cuban newspapers described?

I wiped my sweaty palms on the armrests and pushed Frankie back into his seat.

The cars and roadways underneath us grew larger. The tires screeched as they hit the ground, then the plane roared to a stop.

My heart pounded. We had landed in Miami. But we had no money, no family, no friends here. How would we know where to go? I had studied English since the third grade, but it had never been my favorite subject in school. Would people understand me? Would I understand them?

I leaned back in my seat, thoughts swirling.

I'd always wanted my parents to give me a little more freedom. Now I was about to experience complete independence.

My stomach churned.

❊ ❊ ❊ ❊ ❊

Frankie gripped my hand as we walked through the terminal.

"There they are." Laura pointed to a group of people standing behind a thick rope. "The welcoming committee." She smiled and lowered her voice. "Guess it's better than the Committee for the Defense of the Revolution."

I nodded and looked around. It was nice not to see any soldiers. We continued to walk toward the crowd.

"My mom's godfather, Ernesto, is meeting me. Who's here for you?" Laura asked.

I bit my lip. "Um, we're, um . . ."

"We're meeting our friend George," Frankie said, giving me a smile.

"Oh, that's good." Laura waved at a short, pudgy man and a woman with gray hair pulled into a bun. "There's Ernesto and his wife now." She gave me a quick hug. "I'll see you back home in a couple of months. Good luck, okay?"

"You too," I said as Laura walked into the open arms of Ernesto and his wife.

And with that, another tie to Cuba was gone.

"So, now what?" Frankie asked.

I glanced around. Most people were being hugged and greeted. I could see people rush by, but everyone spoke English so quickly that I could only understand a couple of words.

Two teenage boys joined us as we stood by a row of blue leather chairs, waiting for something to happen. In less than a minute, everyone had seemed to figure out where they were supposed to go, except for us. We only knew to ask for George.

But who were we supposed to ask?

A tall, thin man smoking a cigarette approached us. With his dark brown suit, he looked like he might be going to a business meeting. Maybe he would know about George. I hoped he'd speak English slowly.

"Are you four looking for someone?" he asked us in Spanish.

Before I could answer, one of the teenage boys spoke up. *"¿Usted conoce a George?"*

The man cracked a smile. *"Yo soy* George. I work with Father Walsh and the Catholic Church."

I breathed a sigh of relief. We'd found him. Or better said, he'd found us. And he sounded Cuban, so we could all speak Spanish to each other.

The taller of the two boys shook George's hand. "Nice to meet you. Now, do you know where we're supposed to go from here? Is it a boarding school or something?"

"No, no." He chuckled at some private joke and knelt down to speak to Frankie. "Would you like some gum?" He held out a green pack of gum.

Frankie glanced up at me, then slowly nodded. *"Gracias,"* he said, taking one thin piece.

George smiled and stood up. "The church is doing its very best to give you all a place to stay, but you have to remember that this isn't a vacation." With the cigarette still in his left hand, he motioned for us to follow him. "Let's get your bags and then I'll find out where you're each going."

I hesitated.

He looked back over his shoulder as I stayed holding on to Frankie. "Don't worry, you're safe here."

Safe? How could we really be safe if we were alone, in a strange country? But there was a kindness in George's eyes that told me he would do his best for us. He reminded me of Papá. The way he carried himself.

How he seemed at ease in the huge airport walking among strangers. There was a certain confidence that inspired our trust.

After we got our bags, George made a quick call on a nearby pay phone, and then took us outside to his light green station wagon. It was a sunny day in Miami, exactly the same as in Cuba, but there was a difference. In Cuba, the air seemed to taste sweeter, as if there were mangoes growing nearby or your mother had just cooked your favorite dish. Here, although I was only a couple hundred miles away, everything felt more sterile, like I'd just walked into an office building. The rhythm of life was different, too. The pulsing sound of people speaking Spanish around me, or the music that would surprise your ears as you passed by an open window, was missing. In Miami, the sounds of cars filled the air, but I couldn't get the pulse of the city. I was sure it was there, so maybe I wasn't listening close enough. Maybe I just didn't want to hear.

After we drove a few minutes, much of the landscape seemed to change. The office buildings and shops were replaced with small, flat-roofed houses, and then those houses seemed to fade into flat, empty fields.

George had been talking about American life and telling stories since we'd left the airport, but I couldn't concentrate on his words. I was grateful that we all spoke Spanish, so it wasn't that I couldn't understand. I just couldn't listen. My mind was elsewhere.

"*Permiso,* George," I interrupted, "where did you say we were going again?" I was looking at what seemed to be miles and miles of nothing.

George put out his cigarette in the car ashtray. "Our first stop will be the Kendall facility. It opened up a few months ago."

"Facility?" I asked.

"Don't worry, it may look like army barracks, but the people there will make you and Frankie as comfortable as possible. For right now, it's the only place the church has that can accommodate girls."

Frankie leaned over the front seat. "Mr. George, you said it was for girls, but I'll be staying there too, right? I'm her brother."

"Yes, yes. Boys under twelve stay across the street, in a different camp, but the older boys will go downtown, to the Cuban Home for Boys."

Frankie spun his head toward me and opened his eyes wide.

"But I'll get to see Frankie, right? Even if we're in different buildings?"

George pulled out another cigarette. "Sometimes. They'll explain everything to you. It's all very organized."

My head swirled. How was I supposed to take care of Frankie if we weren't even in the same place? This couldn't be what Mamá and Papá wanted for us.

"I'm sorry. Can't Frankie and I stay together?"

George looked at me in the rearview mirror. "Once we find you a foster family, then maybe. But you have to remember, your parents sent you here for a reason. Now it's up to you to make them proud. You have to be strong."

Be strong. That's what Papá had told me before I left. But he also said to take care of Frankie.

The station wagon pulled into a parking space between two looming gray buildings separated by a narrow road. A woman wearing horn-rimmed glasses stood outside the smaller building's porch entrance.

"Okay, Lucía. This is where you're staying." George pointed to where the lady stood. "Frankie, you'll be across the road over there. I'll walk you over as soon as Lucía gets situated. Just wait for me here."

George stepped out and opened the car door for me.

Frankie pulled my arm. "Don't leave me."

"I'll be right here, Frankie. I'll figure something out so we can be together. Promise." I tried to slide out of the car, but Frankie held on to me.

"But I don't know anyone there. Lucy, please," he whispered.

"C'mon, Frankie. You're a big boy. Let Lucía go," George said.

The woman with the glasses was checking her watch.

I reached out to touch Frankie. "I have to go, but I'll try—"

"Fine!" He pushed my hand away and slumped back into the seat.

"He'll be all right. Give him some time," George said.

Frankie turned his back on me as George closed the door.

"Come, let me introduce you." George carried my suitcase to the building's entrance. "Martha, this is Lucía Álvarez. Lucía, this is Mrs. Eckhart. She'll help get you settled in."

I smiled politely.

"Nice to meet you, Lucía. Now," she said in heavily accented Spanish, "let's find you a bed."

As George strode to the car, I glanced back to see Frankie watching me.

I gave him a small wave. Frankie just kept staring.

I bent down, picked up my bag, and walked into the building with Mrs. Eckhart. For such a large building, it was strangely quiet, as if even sounds got lost inside. The hallway seemed to stretch on for miles. The heavy double doors creaked as they closed behind me. I quickly turned back and looked through the doors' narrow windows. My heart shattered. I could see Frankie's hands splayed against the station wagon's side window as I heard his muffled yell. *"Luuuciiiaaa!"*

Chapter 17

CASTRO ADOPTS BRAINWASHING
—*NEVADA STATE JOURNAL*, JUNE 4, 1961

Rain splattered against the windowpane. In the glow of
lightning flashes, I could see the girls sleeping in the
bunk beds around me. I felt drained, like I'd shed all the
tears my body could produce. But I hadn't been the only
one crying. For about an hour after the lights were
turned off, all I could hear were the echoes of my sobs
from the girls in the other beds. We were all alone . . .
together.

It was well past midnight and, on my first night
away from Frankie, I wondered how he was doing.
He'd always hated thunderstorms. Was he scared? Crying? Maybe the rain had woken him up, too. Did the
boys cry as much as the girls?

The sound of a bell ringing startled me. At some
point, I'd obviously managed to drift off to sleep.

I opened my eyes and sat up. I'd been lucky enough to have been assigned a bed on the far side of the room, next to the wall. From my top bunk, I had a view of the entire place. I watched as a flurry of girls quickly picked up their things and headed out the door in their pajamas.

Angela, the eleven-year-old girl who slept in the bottom bunk, sprang up and tapped my mattress. *"Apúrate,"* she said.

We'd met the day before, and she'd told me her story of coming from Cienfuegos, Cuba, about two months ago. She insisted that once you knew your way around, things at the camp weren't too bad. I stretched and watched as more girls left the room.

"If you don't hurry, there won't be any hot water." She looked over her shoulder at several empty, unmade bunks. *"Ay caramba,* it's too late!" She threw her clothes back on the bed.

"Sorry, I didn't know." I climbed down and pulled my suitcase from under the bed. It was the only place to store my things.

"Yeah," she muttered, "price we pay for having the last bunk. Guess we'll have to shower tomorrow."

"I don't mind taking a cold *ducha.*" I figured a cold one was better than none at all.

"Sure, if you want to miss breakfast, too."

"¿Qué?" I asked.

"Didn't Mrs. Eckhart explain things to you?" Angela rolled her eyes and sighed. "Breakfast is served in the cafeteria at exactly seven-thirty. If you don't get there on time, you won't be able to eat because we have English class right after. Mrs. Eckhart's the teacher. They say she used to teach English at some private school in Havana before the revolution kicked her out."

"Right, she mentioned that yesterday. But after class we get free time, so I can go see my brother at the boys' camp, right?"

Angela shook her head. "Nah, free time means we can go outside, play games, read books. Some girls write to their families. That kinda stuff. They'll bring over the boys for a little while at some point during the day, but that's it."

My shoulders slumped.

"*Oye,* it could be worse. They could've sent your brother to a different camp and you'd only see him on Saturdays."

"*Sí,*" I sighed, "it could always be worse."

❖   ❖   ❖   ❖   ❖

I stood behind Angela, waiting in line to get my breakfast tray. The "cafeteria" was really just a huge room with about twenty small, square tables. An old woman wearing a hairnet and a light blue maid's uniform brought in several trays at a time. The girls in front of me referred to her as Nena.

Angela turned around. "Keep Nena on your good side. If you clean your own tray and you're nice to her, she'll get you a little extra of your favorites."

"Like what?" I asked, eyeing the box of cereal and container of milk sitting on the tray.

"Breakfast is always the same. Don't even dream of *café con leche* or *pan cubano*. They don't have that kinda stuff. But sometimes for dinner she'll give you an extra piece of chicken instead of the vegetables they always want us to eat."

"Oh." I watched as about fifty Cuban girls, of all ages, sat around eating their cereal, laughing and talking about the upcoming day. With everyone speaking Spanish, it almost felt like we were in a boarding school back home.

Yet this wasn't Cuba, and no matter how much I wished that everything was okay, it wasn't. I knew it and all the girls in the room knew it, too.

"Next week you can have my bottom bunk." Angela poured the milk into her bowl.

"*¿Por qué?*" I took a bite of the sweet, crunchy flakes. It wasn't bad, but it tasted like I was having a dessert for breakfast.

"I'm going to live with a family in Oregon. They say the family's got a daughter just about my age. Anyway, it's not like I have a choice."

"Why can't you just stay here?" I asked.

"This place is only temporary." She leaned closer to me. "We're like puppies at the pound. If we don't get picked up by friends or some extended-family member, then they ship us off to make room for the new arrivals."

"But don't parents sometimes come to get their kids?"

Angela took a big sip from the orange juice carton on her tray. "Sure. I heard that happened a couple of months ago to someone, but that was before I got here."

"So, they're sending you to Oregon. Is that far from here?"

"Mmm-hmm. Other side of the country. Above California. But at least I'll be going with Claudia." She pointed to a little girl about eight years old sitting at a table with kids her own age. "And I'll only have to share a room with her, instead of fifty other people. It won't be too bad."

I nodded, but I wasn't sure if she was saying this to convince me or to convince herself.

She slowly exhaled and looked at me. "Your time will come, too."

❊   ❊   ❊   ❊   ❊

Classes at the camp reminded me of school in Cuba, except here there was a sense of urgency in learning English. The idea of having to speak a foreign language all the time was overwhelming, even for girls like me who'd studied English for years. Back home, I used to feel worldly being able to understand the American movies and songs, but now I just felt silly speaking in English. Thankfully, everyone else around me sounded just like me or a little worse.

"All right, ladies . . . class is dismissed. Please

remember to practice speaking to each other in English. It will help you outside of camp." Mrs. Eckhart stood at the door and handed each of us a list with vocabulary words. "Read over these new terms and we will discuss them all tomorrow. Enjoy the rest of your day, girls."

I walked back to the central yard and glanced down at the purple-inked paper. It still had the smell of the mimeograph machine that it had been printed on.

"Lucy!"

I looked over at the picnic table and saw Frankie sitting with a few other boys. He quickly swung his legs over the bench and ran toward me.

"Lucy, we've got to figure out a way to go back home," he said, hugging me tightly.

"Frankie, you know we can't."

"Then can't you make them let me stay here with you?"

"They won't let you, but we'll see each other every afternoon."

"That's not good enough. I don't know how things are over here, but it's horrible over there." He pointed across the road.

I pushed him back a little and looked at him from head to toe. "Did something happen?"

"Nah, a couple of bullies tried to mess with me, but I'm tough and it's no big deal. But the food is really bad, Lucy." He gave me a pained look.

I started laughing.

"No, really. I'm not kidding. I'm starving."

I shook my head. Leave it to Frankie to view everything through his stomach.

"Can't you do something to get us home? Maybe we can call and Papá can send money to fly back?"

"No."

"What if we sneak out and stow away on a plane back to Cuba?"

"No."

"Well, if we do something really bad and they kick us out of the camp, then they'd have to—"

"Don't even think about it, Frankie," I warned. "We *will* make Mamá and Papá proud. Mrs. Eckhart already sent a telegram to them saying that we were staying here. We'll probably get letters from Mamá and Papá soon."

"Not soon enough," Frankie muttered.

"Look, this isn't fun for anyone, but I'll figure something out. We still have each other, and some kids get sent to foster homes. Maybe we'll end up with a really nice family somewhere in Miami Beach."

Frankie crossed his arms and looked away. "Yeah, or we'll end up in a place where they'll turn us into slaves, make us sleep on the floor, and feed us dog food."

"Frankie, you know that won't happen."

"Fine, but they could separate us. Send us to different homes. That really does happen. Did you think about that?"

I opened my mouth to answer but realized that there was nothing to say. He was right. It could happen.

"See, we have to do something before it's too late."

"I'll figure something out, Frankie. I promise." I looked around. Some girls had started to play badminton, and a few others were reading under the shadow cast by one of the buildings. "C'mon, I'll show you around. I think they even have some board games in the main hall."

Frankie shrugged.

I gave him a little nudge. "Challenge you to a game of checkers."

"Ha, challenge?" He smirked. "You've never beaten me."

"We'll see. Things are different now."

Chapter 18

SCHOOL LAW APPROVED; CUBA TAKES OVER
SCHOOL FACILITIES
—*THE NEW YORK TIMES*, JUNE 8, 1961

It was my fifth day at Kendall. I felt like a prisoner, counting the days of a sentence, waiting for my release. The only good moments were when I got to see Frankie, but other than that, I just couldn't get used to life at the camp. There was never any real privacy, and we weren't allowed to leave the area surrounding the girls' camp. Not that there would be anywhere to go. We were in the middle of nowhere, surrounded by a scattering of trees that housed millions of mosquitoes, and they seemed to be the only visitors we got.

"Good night, Lucía." A couple of voices called out in the dwindling light. The sun had gone down about fifteen minutes earlier, and since the lights were always turned off at exactly eight o'clock, most girls were already in their assigned beds, chatting until total darkness set in.

"*Hasta mañana,*" I answered as I walked past the rows and rows of bunk beds. I had chosen to change in the bathroom so I could have a little bit of privacy, and now I was one of the last ones getting into the room.

I thought about Mamá and Papá. Back home, we'd usually be finishing dinner at around this time. Were they eating right now? Would they spend the rest of the evening outside on the porch, trying to keep up appearances? When would I get a letter from them? I knew that all the mail was checked and read by the Cuban censors, but how much longer would it take?

As I approached my bunk, Angela rolled over to face me. In the dim room, I could see she was waiting for me to get closer.

"Psst, Lucía," she said. "I have something for you."

"*¿Qué?*"

"I took an extra one. You really need to be here on time." She handed me a large sugar cookie and a carton of milk.

"Thanks." I tossed the carton and cookie up onto my bunk and took two steps up the ladder.

Even though Angela was younger, she reminded me a little of Ivette. They both always looked out for me. I peered in between the rungs, down at Angela lying in her bed.

"Good night, Angela. *Te voy a extrañar.*"

"I'm going to miss you, too, Lucía. Good night."

I climbed up to my bed and looked around for the cookie, to make sure I didn't smash it as I crawled in, but it was gone. Had it bounced to the floor? I glanced down, but the floor was bare.

Then the covers moved. Something was there. I was about to scream when I heard a familiar "shhh."

I pulled back the rough gray sheet completely. Frankie lay there grinning from ear to ear, eating my cookie.

For a moment, I was glad to see him, then I realized what he'd done. I glanced around to see if anyone else had seen him. The nightly crying had already started, and everyone was too lost in their own memories to pay attention to me.

"What are you doing here?" I whispered, hoping that the whirring fans overhead would drown out my voice.

He pulled the cover back up over his head, only letting a small corner of his face show. "I had to see you. Lucy, I can't take it anymore. I want to go home."

I crawled into bed, pushing him against the wall. "You know we can't, Frankie."

"Lucía, is that you? Are you talking to yourself?" Angela asked from below.

"Yeah, sorry. I was, um, I was just praying."

"Oh, okay. No problem."

I signaled for Frankie to keep it down.

He lowered his voice some more. "I won't stay here,

The memory of his footsteps sounded so real that they could have been right next to me. I turned over, and through half-closed eyelids I saw two shadowy figures by my bunk.

"Mamá? Papá?" I muttered.

"There you are!" a woman's voice grumbled as a large hand pulled Frankie by the leg.

Chapter 19

KHRUSHCHEV TOLD KENNEDY HE FEELS
CUBA'S CASTRO IS UNSTABLE
—*THE LINCOLN EVENING JOURNAL*, JUNE 8, 1961

"We can't have boys sneaking into the girls' dormitory. All the young ladies deserve to feel safe. We owe them that much!" Mrs. Eckhart argued.

"I know, I know." Mr. Ramírez nodded. "But he's only seven and he wanted to be with his sister. You can understand that."

Frankie and I sat next to each other in a small office watching the two administrators go back and forth deciding what our punishment should be.

Mrs. Eckhart walked over to me, and in her heavily accented Spanish she tried to explain the problem. "We simply cannot have unsupervised boys entering the girls' building. You're a young lady now. Imagine if someone else's brother were to come in . . . get into your bed. How do I know he won't do this again?"

"I won't. Promise." Frankie gave her his sad-puppy-dog eyes.

Mr. Ramírez raised his eyebrows. "*Oye,* that's what you told me the last four times I caught you sneaking out."

"*¿Cuatro?*" I asked.

Frankie shrugged and dropped his head.

"It's become a pattern, except tonight he wasn't caught until he'd snuck into the girls' building. Mr. Ramírez, I don't think there's any other choice. He needs to be sent to the Cuban Home for Boys."

"No!" Frankie yelled.

"Wait, where is that? Isn't that far away?" I stood up. "That'll mean we won't get to see each other except on Saturdays."

"Lucía, we've tried, and Frankie knew there'd be consequences." Mr. Ramírez shook his head. "He'll be well cared for over there, and as soon as a foster family becomes available, we'll reunite you."

I slumped back into my chair. "Frankie, what have you done?"

Frankie jumped up and put his hands on his hips. "If you send me away, I won't stay there. I'll just run away again. I want to be with Lucía!"

I pulled him down by his elbow. He was making things worse.

Mrs. Eckhart threw her hands up. "This is why I oversee the girls and not the boys," she muttered.

"Please," I begged, "give him another chance. I'll help. He won't do it again."

Mr. Ramírez's face softened.

"It's just that in Puerto Mijares we were never really apart." My voice shook.

Mrs. Eckhart shook her head. "I'm sorry, Lucía. I have to think of the facility's reputation and what's best for all the girls."

"Puerto Mijares? That's where you're from?" Mr. Ramírez asked.

I nodded as I tried to think of something else to convince them to let Frankie stay.

"Wait a minute. Lucía Álvarez? Are you related to Fernando Álvarez?" Mr. Ramírez searched my face as if trying to see a resemblance.

"He's my father," I said.

He shook his head in disbelief. "*¡Increíble!* The last time I saw your father, you were only four or five years old." He turned to Mrs. Eckhart. "Lucía's father is the one I told you about. Why I took this job. That man helped me when I had no money. He even paid for the medicines that my youngest needed."

Mrs. Eckhart smiled at me. "Sounds like your father is a very special person."

Mr. Ramírez placed his hands on Frankie's shoulders. "He didn't even want to be repaid. Said that someday I'd help another child and that'd be repayment enough." He paused to look at Frankie and me. "Martha, we can't separate them."

Hope filled my heart. Frankie just crossed his arms and kept the defiant look in his eye.

"But we can't make an exception. It wouldn't be fair to the other children and . . ." Mrs. Eckhart faced Frankie. "I'm sorry, I just don't trust that you'll follow the rules."

Mr. Ramírez snapped his fingers. "I've got it! What if they take the place of Barbara and José Camacho? They left with a relative this morning, so we have an opening with the Baxter family."

Mrs. Eckhart pursed her lips. "It's not the way things are normally done . . . we have a process."

"What's normal these days?" Mr. Ramírez paused, gauging Mrs. Eckhart's reaction. "Martha, I owe it to their father. It's the least I can do."

My heart pounded. This might be our only chance.

Mrs. Eckhart gave a slight nod, relenting.

"¡Perfecto! Now you two can stay together, but the flight is scheduled for this morning and—"

"We'll do it!" I said.

"Yes, but you should know a few things," Mr. Ramírez added.

"¿Qué?" I waited for the catch. There was always a catch.

"Most of the foster families live in different parts of the country and speak very little Spanish."

"I know." I looked at Mrs. Eckhart. "Are we going to Oregon like Angela?" I dreaded the idea of living so far away from Cuba, in a cold place, but at least Frankie and I would be together.

"Oh no. Not that far away. This family lives near Grand Island, Nebraska." Mr. Ramírez glanced over at Mrs. Eckhart. "That reminds me, we'll have to contact the Baxters, let them know about the change." Mr. Ramírez gave me a wink. "But I'm sure there won't be a problem. You're in agreement with all of this, right, Lucía?"

"Sí," I said, although inside I was trying to remember where Nebraska was on the map. I thought it was one of the states in the middle of the country, but if we were going to an island, then it had to be on the coast. Maybe it would look like Cuba.

"You're good with this, too, Frankie?" Mr. Ramírez dropped to one knee and looked Frankie squarely in the eye. "Remember that you'll be a guest in their home. No funny business. I don't want to hear any complaints, because I won't be able to help you again, *¿comprendes?"*

Frankie smiled. "If I can be with Lucy and take care of her, then I'll be okay."

I shook my head. *Frankie, my hero.*

"All right, it's settled. I'll take care of the paperwork and sending a telegram to your parents telling them of the change. Mrs. Eckhart will make sure you go back to your own beds and get a few more hours of sleep. You can pack your bags right after breakfast."

I stifled a laugh. Pack? There wasn't anyone at the camp who had ever unpacked.

❀　❀　❀　❀　❀

"I can't believe you're leaving before me," Angela muttered as she scooped up the last of her cereal. "You going to eat that?" She pointed to my untouched toast.

"No, I'm not really hungry." I slid the plate toward her.

Most of the girls in the dining hall were finishing their breakfasts and dropping off their trays at the door. Classes were about to start, and another day of waiting, waiting for real life to begin, lay ahead.

"Are you excited?" Angela asked.

"I don't know. It's happening so fast, I'm not sure how I feel." I stirred my soggy cereal.

"I think it's great. You said it's an island, right? Maybe their house will be on the beach. Plus, don't you want to be with your brother?"

"Of course. It's just, well, who knows what these people are like. Besides, here everyone else is like us."

"I'm sure they're nice. Why else would they agree to take you in?"

I stayed quiet. Frankie's fears about being slaves suddenly didn't seem so far-fetched.

"Look, I've got to get to class. You've got my address in Cuba. When we're back home, write to me and tell me how your summer went. I'll let you know all about Oregon, okay?" Angela walked around the table and gave me a hug.

"Sure, maybe you can come to my *quinces* in November."

"Yeah, I'd like that."

"*Cuídate*, Angela," I said as she picked up her tray.

"You take care, too. See you in Cuba."

Chapter 20

CUBA, BERLIN PRESENT LONG-TERM WOES
—*THE HERALD-PRESS*, JUNE 9, 1961

The crisp ten-dollar bill crinkled as I reached into my purse for my boarding ticket. Mr. Ramírez had given us the money before we left the camp. It was the first time I'd been given any American money. Between this and the boxes of cigars that Papá had given us before we left, I felt rich.

I adjusted my yellow headband and glanced up at the large clock on the airport wall. We'd been waiting in Chicago for our connecting flight for about three hours. I still wasn't sure where Grand Island was, and I'd been too embarrassed to ask anyone at the camp.

I began to imagine the sea air, sand, and small fishing boats . . . like in Puerto Mijares. But even if it wasn't exactly like Cuba, at least it was an island, and no matter where you went in the world, an island was still an island.

My thoughts continued to swirl when I noticed two men walk by with trench coats draped over their arms. Immediately I sat up and clutched my purse. Frankie and I had heard stories about Chicago, and I'd seen movies about Al Capone and the mob. My heartbeat quickened as one of the men stopped and doubled back toward us. He paused in front of a small kiosk, bought a newspaper, then continued down the terminal.

I breathed a sigh of relief. It was silly for me to imagine mobsters lurking around, but still, I was happy we'd found seats against the airport wall . . . just in case.

❁　❁　❁　❁　❁

The airport in Nebraska was empty compared to the ones in Miami, Chicago . . . even Havana.

"Hey, is that for us?" Frankie pointed to a petite older woman with short blond hair who held a cardboard sign with the words LUCÍA AND FRANCISCO ÁLVAREZ written on it.

"Must be," I said.

The woman waved at us and said something to the large man behind her. He seemed less than happy to be at the airport, but he followed her as she walked over to us.

"You two must be Lucía and Francisco." She gave us a big smile that showed all her teeth. "I just knew it had to be you. Wearing those pretty linen clothes. Nothing like that around here." She threw open her arms like a magician's assistant. "Well, I guess this is . . . welcome to America!"

"*Gracias,* um, thank you." I smiled politely.

"Oh, you speak English, that's good. I was worried that you wouldn't understand me. So, do you have any questions? Ha, listen to me." She looked back at the large man, who had yet to even crack the slightest smile. "I haven't even introduced us. This is Mr. Baxter, and I'm Mrs. Baxter. We're your foster family."

"*Yo soy* Frankie."

Mrs. Baxter shook his hand and laughed. "Well, I certainly didn't think you were Lucía!"

Mr. Baxter gave us both a nod, then checked his watch.

"So, do you have many bags?" Mrs. Baxter asked. "I expect you don't. I've read some horrible things about what's been happening in Cuba. You must be so happy to be out of there. Oh, I can't imagine living like that. In all that fear. You'll be safe with us till your parents can get out of Cuba. Did you tell me how many bags you brought?"

"*¡Esta mujer habla más que un cao!*" Frankie whispered.

He was right . . . she did talk a lot. What was worse, she was speaking so quickly that I had no idea what she was saying. I heard *blah, blah, blabbity, blah,* Cuba, then some more *blabbity blah.*

"I sorry. I no understand," I said in my best broken English.

"Oh, you *don't* know English. Why didn't you say so before? I guess I've just been rambling on a bit." She pointed to the floor and said in a loud voice, "This . . . is . . . Lincoln. We . . . go . . ."—she pointed outside— "to . . . Grand . . . Island. Our . . . home."

Frankie and I giggled. I liked her more when she talked fast.

"I speak a little English. We happy to be here."

"Good. I'll just talk a little slower, then. I seem to speak quickly when I get excited. Well, like I was saying, you're safe here, and you don't have to worry about going back to Cuba."

Not go back to Cuba? Did she think we were staying here for good? I thought about the correct words to say.

"No, we go back to Cuba soon. When things get better, then Mamá and Papá send for us," I explained.

"Well, we can certainly hope. Now, let's go get your things and head home. Mr. Baxter likes to have dinner by five o'clock."

"Humpf," Mr. Baxter muttered. It was the only thing he'd said so far.

❀   ❀   ❀   ❀   ❀

As we drove from the airport and got onto the highway, I realized that it didn't seem like we were anywhere near water. In fact, from the airplane all I'd seen were green fields. I wondered how long before we reached the coast and if maybe I should've gone to the bathroom before leaving.

"How much time to Grand Island?" I asked.

"Oh, 'bout an hour and a half. *Noventa* minutes." Mrs. Baxter winked and nudged Mr. Baxter. "See, I remember a little of my high school Spanish. I can still say any number from one to a hundred."

Mr. Baxter kept his eyes on the road ahead.

I was surprised at how much English I actually understood when she spoke more slowly. The years of required English classes at school were finally paying off. "We take boat to island?" I asked, envisioning a ferry like the ones I'd seen in some magazines.

Mr. Baxter glanced back at me as if I'd just come from Mars.

"Boat?" Mrs. Baxter chuckled. "Oh my, you thought it was an island because of its name." She looked back from her seat in the Ford Fairlane to face me. "No island, no water. Just cornfields."

I gave her a blank look.

She pointed out the open window to the little green stalks growing on either side of the road. "See . . . corn. No island."

"*¿Eso es maíz?*" Frankie asked.

"Yes, corn. Now you say it, Frankie. Corn."

"*Repítelo,*" I told Frankie.

"Corn," he repeated.

"Good. That's our first English lesson. What better word to learn first? Tomorrow we'll start a full day of English classes. By the time school starts, the two of you will be talking up a storm." Mrs. Baxter turned back around and spoke to her husband. "You know, I always wanted to be a teacher when I was growing up in Minnesota."

"Hmm," he answered.

I watched as the minutes went by and the flat green fields never ended. The road stretched out for miles and miles without a town or intersection to break up the monotony of the scenery. That, combined with the slight rumbling of the car, had already put Frankie to sleep. His head leaned against the side door. I looked out my window and wondered what Mamá and Papá were doing in Cuba right then. Was Papá out trying to find work? Were they still being watched? Would they get involved with the underground or try to fit in with the new system? Were they thinking of ways for us to be able to return home? Could it be we'd never go back? Would we be stuck here forever?

Chapter 21

NEXT MOVE IS FIDEL CASTRO'S, IN "CHESS GAME"
—*THE COSHOCTON TRIBUNE*, JUNE 9, 1961

"This will be your room, Lucía. It was my son Carl's room until he got married and moved to Boston."

I walked into a small bedroom with dark wood panels on the walls. A faded blue quilt lay folded neatly at the foot of the bed, and a desk was placed under the only window. I gazed outside and saw an empty field.

"Yes, our fields are bare. Mr. Baxter hurt his back a couple of months ago, and we missed the corn-planting season. Lucky for us, my brother gave him a job at the feed store in town so we can make ends meet until it's time for the winter wheat."

I touched the small lamp on the desk.

"Thank you. Is very nice," I said.

"*It* is very nice. We need to start improving your English." Mrs. Baxter smiled and pointed to the hallway.

Cuban food. Even at the camp, they kept giving us salads and all these vegetables. At home, we'd have yuca or potatoes, but most of our vegetables were cooked with something else. Like in a stew or as flavoring for the main dish. I was craving *picadillo*, rice, black beans, *café con leche*, Cuban bread, and most of all, Mamá's *flan*.

"Come, Lucía, help me clear the table. Frankie, you can go play until bedtime." Mrs. Baxter picked up the water pitcher as Mr. Baxter dropped off his plate in the kitchen and went outside.

Frankie stared at me, waiting for me to translate.

"Puedes ir a jugar," I said.

"Wait. Lucía, how do you say go play?" Mrs. Baxter asked.

"Ve a jugar."

"Okay, Frankie. *Vay a who-gar*. Go play." She pointed to him. "Now you."

"Go play," Frankie repeated.

Mrs. Baxter grinned. "Wonderful. You're going to be such a fast learner, I can just tell!"

Frankie shrugged and ran off to his room.

I stacked a few plates and followed Mrs. Baxter into the wallpapered kitchen. It was a medley of yellow and green flowers on the walls, with mustard-colored appliances.

"Thank you, Lucía." She took the plates and put them in the sink.

"You're welcome."

"It's so nice that you know some English. Ever since Carl left home, it's been so quiet around here." She picked up a sponge and gave me a dry towel. "But I already told you about him. Tell me a little about where you're from. Where is *Porto Mee-ja-rays*?"

"*Me-ha-res*. It is east of Havana. On a bitch," I explained.

"Oh my! No! Never say that. Look at me." She pointed to her lips. "Be-e-each. Now you."

"Be-e-each," I said, contorting my mouth into the same huge smile she had.

"Good. Well, what about your house. Big like this one or little?"

I looked around at the small house. Our home in Cuba was twice as big.

"More big. Not so much land."

"Bigger, not *more big*." She continued to wash the dishes and pass them to me to dry. "And your father, what does he do for a living?"

"He work at the bank." I remembered the soldiers taking Papá from our house. "But *la revolución* no let him work now."

"Oh, that Fidel is just destroying your country. He's a Communist, I tell you, no doubt in my mind."

I continued drying the dishes, unsure of what I was supposed to say.

After a few minutes, when we were done, I asked Mrs. Baxter if we could call my parents in Cuba.

"I'm afraid that's very expensive. Why don't you write to them?" she offered while taking off her apron and hanging it behind the pantry door. "Mr. Baxter and I can give you and Frankie fifty cents every week as an allowance." She glanced up at the ceiling as if retrieving a distant memory. "It's just like when Carl was young." Mrs. Baxter then looked back down at me. "You'll both be given responsibilities around the house, but we'll also give you certain liberties. For instance, you can spend your allowance on anything you like, including stamps, but there'll be limits, of course."

I reached into my skirt pocket and pulled out the ten-dollar bill. "I have some money."

"So I see, but calling Cuba may cost more than that. You can save up your allowance, and when you've got enough, we'll make the call."

"We have two boxes of cigars, too. We sell those and have more money." I wanted, no, I needed to make that call.

She smiled and went to the cupboard. "I'll have Mr. Baxter take the boxes into town on Monday to see what he can get for them." She pulled down a small blue jar. "Here, put your money in this." She took the lid off and waited for me to put the bill inside. "We'll call it your 'Calls to Cuba Fund.' Whatever the calls cost, we'll take the money from here. But if there's no money, there'll be no calls." She reached up and put the blue jar on the top shelf. "It's not that we don't want you to talk to your parents, we just can't afford it right now."

My heart sank. I'd have to wait.

"*Está bien* . . . I mean, okay."

❀   ❀   ❀   ❀   ❀

"They seem nice, Lucy. I'm glad we're here," Frankie said, playing with a few toy soldiers on the floor of my room.

"Uh-huh." I concentrated on the letter I was writing to Mamá and Papá. It had to be a balance between telling them where we were, finding out what was happening at home, and still not writing anything that might get them into trouble if the soldiers were to read the mail.

I read what I'd written so far.

> Dear Mamá and Papá,
>
> First, let me say that Frankie and I are fine. We've been sent to live with the Baxters in Grand Island, Nebraska. They are a nice older Catholic couple. I think we will be happier here than at the camp because we are together now. I know in my earlier letters I didn't mention the fact that Frankie and I were staying at different camps, but the camps were across the street from each other and I didn't want to worry you.
>
> How are things for you? Has Tío Antonio

come by again? Do you think we'll be home soon? When?

Mrs. Baxter walked into my room. "I see you like the toys, Frankie. But it's almost eight o'clock and you two need to go to bed."

I looked up from my desk. It was still light outside. Did everyone in America go to bed this early?

"Now, remember that the toothbrushes I bought for you are in the medicine cabinet, right next to Mr. Baxter's shaving cream on the bottom shelf." She walked over to Frankie and placed her hand on his back to coax him out of my room. "You'll translate for him, won't you, Lucía?"

I nodded. "*Que los cepillos de dientes están en el gabinete al lado de la crema de afeitar del señor Baxter.*"

"I really am delighted to have the two of you here with us," Mrs. Baxter said as she guided Frankie toward the door. "Tomorrow we'll have our first full day together. I'll wake you both up so you can help Mr. Baxter with the chickens."

Frankie stared up at her. "Chee-kens?"

"Yes, you know, chickens. *Bawk, bawk, bawk.*" She flapped her arms.

Frankie giggled and whispered over to me in Spanish, "I think she wants to make chicken for dinner tomorrow night." He turned to her and said in his best English, "Me like chee-ken."

"Well, that's a healthy work attitude." Mrs. Baxter ushered him toward his bedroom. "Now skedaddle. I want lights out in two minutes. So good night and I'll see you at dawn."

Work? Dawn? Suddenly I didn't think Frankie was right about the chickens just being our dinner.

Chapter 22

CASTRO SET TO SWAP MAN FOR MACHINE
—*THE RENO EVENING GAZETTE*, JUNE 10, 1961

I lifted the basket of eggs onto the kitchen counter. The sun was just starting to peek above the horizon.

"*¡Qué frío!*" Frankie said, rubbing his arms through his sweater.

I took off my coat. It *was* cold outside . . . really cold. And to think that the day before, it'd been warm, almost like in Cuba.

"You're wearing your new coat? To feed the chickens?" Mrs. Baxter asked.

I shrugged. What else was I supposed to wear? I knew it was summer, but it had to be in the fifties outside. Plus, the coat had protected me from the chickens' pecking.

Mrs. Baxter took a few of the eggs and cracked them into a large bowl. "I guess the mornings are a bit cooler here than what you're used to. I'll get you one of my sweaters for tomorrow, because you'll want to save that coat for when it really gets cold in the winter."

"*¿Qué dice?*" Frankie asked.

I explained that she was getting me a sweater because the coat was for the winter.

"*¿A cuanto baja en el invierno?*"

"Mrs. Baxter, Frankie wants to know how cold winter is." I took a seat at the small table next to the refrigerator.

She whisked the eggs and poured them into a skillet on the stove. "Pretty cold . . . I'd say somewhere in the teens." Mrs. Baxter wiped her hands on her apron. "I guess you'll be seeing snow for the first time. How do you say 'snow' in Spanish?"

"*Nieve,* but we not be here too long," I said.

Mrs. Baxter faced Frankie and started some sort of sign language. "You . . . here." She pointed at the ground. "See"—she touched her eyes—"*nee-ay-vay.*"

Frankie jumped out of his chair. "*Hoy? Nieve?*" He raced toward the window, almost crashing into Mr. Baxter as he came in through the back door.

"Oh no, not today." Mrs. Baxter laughed. "In winter."

"*En el invierno, bobo,*" I explained.

Frankie turned around and stuck his tongue out at me for calling him stupid.

Mr. Baxter grumbled something as he sat down at the table.

"Here you go. Eggs, bacon, and toast." She placed a plate in front of Mr. Baxter.

I eyed his food. It looked good.

"And this is for you and Frankie." She put down identical plates in front of us. "I bought this at the market last week. I thought you might want to add it to the eggs." She pulled out a little red bottle from the pocket of her apron.

I watched to see if Mr. or Mrs. Baxter would use it, but they didn't. At home, I'd never put anything on my eggs, but I wondered if it would be rude not to try it.

Mrs. Baxter sat in front of me and took a bite of her toast. "Go ahead. It's a little taste from home. The brand may be different, but I'm sure it's similar to what you usually eat."

Frankie watched me open the bottle and pour some of the red sauce next to the eggs. Carefully I dipped some egg into it. Mrs. Baxter smiled, waiting for my reaction.

I took a bite.

Instantly my tongue was on fire. I swallowed the eggs without chewing and grabbed the glass of juice sitting on the table. I didn't stop drinking until about half of the glass was gone.

Frankie giggled.

"Oh my, you don't like it?" Mrs. Baxter's eyebrows were scrunched together. "I thought you liked spicy food. I read that in Mexico they put it on everything, even their eggs."

"Ughmm." I cleared my throat. "In Cuba, we no eat spicy food. Mexico yes, Cuba no." Even my ears felt hot.

"Oh." Mrs. Baxter looked disappointed. "Well, in that case, just eat the breakfast without the Tabasco sauce. We'll start with your English lessons right after we clean up. Yes?"

I understood something about eating without tobacco and having English class. I nodded in agreement.

Mr. Baxter wiped his mouth and stood up. "Good breakfast, Helen," he said, and bent down to give his wife a peck on the cheek.

It was the first time I'd heard him speak. I didn't even know Mrs. Baxter's first name was Helen.

"Thank you, dear. I'll see you after work."

"Humpf," Mr. Baxter muttered as he walked out the back door.

Mrs. Baxter faced me again. "He hates having to go into the feed store on Saturdays, but at least it's only until one. He just can't wait to get back to the land."

I nodded.

"And tonight is a big night. Lawrence Welk is on TV. All the singing, dancing, and polka music. You'll love it!"

I wasn't sure who this Lawrence Welk was, but if she was this excited about him being on TV, then I figured he was probably very similar to Elvis.

Chapter 23

TRACTORS-FOR-FREEDOM TEAM GOING TO HAVANA
—*THE LINCOLN EVENING JOURNAL*, JUNE 12, 1961

After only a few days of being with the Baxters, I was exhausted. Not from any of the chores we'd been given, although living on a farm was much harder than I'd imagined. It was that I'd grown tired of constantly keeping a watchful eye on Frankie. I tried to keep him from speaking too loudly, running through the house, or chewing with his mouth open. I reminded him that we were visitors in the Baxter home and could be sent away at any time. If that happened, we'd most likely be separated.

"Bet you can't catch me," Frankie laughed as he ran around me.

"Not now." I was concentrating on avoiding the large mud puddles left behind after the strong morning storm. "Can't you see I'm working? Why don't you help me carry this bag of feed over to the shed? The faster I finish, the sooner we can go eat lunch."

"Put it down." He poked me in the ribs. "Look. I can jump over that *charco de fango* without getting dirty." He ran ahead and leapt over the mud puddle. He circled it and came back to me.

"Your turn, Lucy. See if you can jump it."

"Frankie, behave."

"Go. I'll hold all that chicken food." He reached for the brown canvas sack.

"No. It's open on the top."

"I got it. Now try to make it over." Frankie pulled on the bag and tried to shove me aside.

"Watch it!" I yelled, but it was too late. I lost my grip on the bag and felt myself slip on the wet earth.

All the grain spilled out of the bag and fell on the muddy ground. I tried to keep my balance, but my penny loafers had no grip, and a second later I lay in the mud, too, my flowered dress splattered with gunk.

"Ha, ha, ha!" Frankie doubled over with laughter. "You look like a pig sitting there."

I glared at him. "Shut up." I stared at the wasted feed. The Baxters would not be happy.

Frankie kept laughing, almost unable to breathe.

I couldn't stand it. I grabbed a handful of brown muck and slung it at him, hitting him squarely in the nose.

The shock on Frankie's face made me giggle.

Frankie stood there staring at me.

I laughed harder.

This, for Frankie, was a declaration of war, and he grabbed his own handful of mud to throw at me.

I raised my hand. "Don't," I warned.

"Or what?" he said.

"Or I'll"—I grabbed another handful and tossed it at his shirt—"do this again."

Frankie smiled and flung the mud he was holding, hitting me on the shoulder.

For the next couple of minutes, Frankie and I attacked each other mercilessly. We slapped each other with the muddy mix of dirt, water, and chicken feed. Sliding around the sludge, I tried to grab Frankie by the waist, only to have him spin out of my hands and land with a splat in a larger mud puddle. Our squeals of laughter riled up the chickens, and soon they were flapping their wings, shrieking along with us.

"Lucía! Frankie! What are you doing?"

Mrs. Baxter stood on the back porch watching us make a mess of each other.

I looked at Frankie, covered head to toe in mud. I was in the same condition.

"*Ay*, Frankie. *¿Qué hemos hecho?* She's going to think we're savages," I whispered.

Frankie hung his head and lowered his shoulders. We bent down and tried to put a bit of the clean grain back into the sack.

"Leave that alone and come over here," Mrs. Baxter called out.

We slowly walked toward the house like dogs about to get a beating.

As we got closer, I noticed Mrs. Baxter had something behind her back. When we were only about ten feet away, she whipped out a green hose and aimed it at us. "Time to wash up!"

I didn't know whether to laugh or be scared. Mrs. Baxter started to chuckle as she unfolded the kink in the hose and water sprayed out. She took aim at Frankie, who ran around avoiding the water. I laughed at the silliness of it all until she pointed the hose at me. Then I ran along with Frankie and laughed some more. I didn't stop until the pain in my side forced me to take a long, deep breath.

❊   ❊   ❊   ❊   ❊

After changing out of our wet clothes and having lunch, Frankie and I helped Mrs. Baxter peel some potatoes for the night's dinner. The three of us sitting quietly around the kitchen table reminded me of days spent helping Mamá in Cuba. There was a sense of peace in what we were doing. Maybe it wasn't so much in our actions but from the fact that most of the tension that I'd carried with me to Nebraska had been washed away by Mrs. Baxter's green hose.

The ringing phone pulled me away from my thoughts, and Mrs. Baxter rushed to the living room to answer it.

Frankie voiced my own wish. "Maybe it's Mamá and Papá calling."

I didn't answer since I wasn't sure if they even knew the phone number of where we were staying.

"Lucía." Mrs. Baxter walked back into the kitchen. "That was Mr. Baxter on the phone. He says he was able to sell both boxes of cigars, for ten dollars each, so we'll place that call to your parents tonight."

"Can we call now?" I asked.

"No, honey. I think it's better if we wait for Mr. Baxter. Apparently, it's a bit more complicated than just dialing the number. Something about having to make the call through another country and then waiting for a phone line to Cuba to become available."

"Oh."

"He'll be home soon, though. Why don't we take a break from these potatoes and work on your English for a while?" Mrs. Baxter picked up the bowl of peeled potatoes and placed it on the kitchen counter. "Lucía, you can read the newspaper that's out in the living room, and, Frankie"—she pulled out a picture book from one of the kitchen drawers—"we can read another book."

Frankie rolled his eyes at me. "*Yo se leer.* Why do I have to look at baby books?"

"You don't know how to read or speak in English. *Presta atención,*" I answered.

"*Está bien.* I'll pay attention, but I won't need any of this stuff when we go back home."

Mrs. Baxter let out a little nervous laugh as she placed the book in front of Frankie. "I'm not sure what you two are saying, but I hope it's all good."

"Yes, everything good, Mrs. Baxter. Frankie just not like to study much."

"Well, this is just the beginning. We have to get you two ready for school in September."

I was about to explain that we would be home before school started, but then realized that I really didn't know when we were leaving.

Frankie pointed to a picture on the cover of the book of a birthday cake with lots of candles.

"All right, Frankie, that is a picture of a cake. See the letters underneath. C-A-K-E. Cake." Mrs. Baxter waited for Frankie to repeat the word.

I smiled as I walked out of the kitchen and heard Frankie say, "Cake. Me like cake."

Chapter 24

EX-ENVOY TO CUBA SAYS U.S. SHOULD TRY BLOCKADE
—*THE BRAINERD DAILY DISPATCH*, JUNE 13, 1961

In a dreamlike trance, I pulled the gray wool sweater over my head. I still wasn't used to the early morning routine of going outside to gather the eggs and feed the chickens, but it seemed to be a small price to pay for having Frankie and me be together. Plus, I wanted to help the Baxters, and I'd become quite good at collecting the eggs without getting the chickens all riled up.

Just as I slipped on my penny loafers, a phone rang and disturbed the quiet stillness of the house. A call before sunrise could only mean one thing . . . our call to Cuba had been connected. My parents were on the line.

I raced out of my room to see Mrs. Baxter already talking on the phone.

"Yes, we did place the call. Go ahead and connect me." She waved me over and thrust the receiver into my open hand. "It's the call to your parents," she whispered.

I grabbed the phone like a relay racer taking the baton. There was not a second to lose.

"Mamá? Papá?" I said, expecting to hear their glorious voices.

I only heard a distant crackling noise. No one was on the line.

My heart pounded. I waited. A half second later, the voice I'd been longing to hear was there.

"*¿Hola?* Lucía?"

It was Papá!

Tears filled my eyes. It was so good to hear his voice. To be able to think and speak in Spanish and not worry about translating my thoughts.

"*Sí, ¡estoy aquí!* I'm here!" I called out.

"*¡Mi hija!* We miss you so much. How are you? How's Frankie?"

I blinked and a heavy tear dropped onto my cheek. "We're fine. We're living on a farm in Nebraska."

"*Sí, sí.* We received the telegram from Alfredo Ramírez in Miami. What a small world that he would be in charge of where you were sent! But tell me, how are the Americans treating you? Are they a nice family?"

"The Baxters are very nice. We're learning English. How are you and Mamá?"

"*¿Nosotros? Perfecto,* now that we know you are safe. Hold on . . . your mother wants to talk to you. *Te quiero,* Lucy."

"Love you too, Papá."

I heard him give my mother the phone with instructions to speak quickly because the call was expensive.

I brushed away the tear that was now clinging to the bottom of my chin. "Mamá?"

"Lucía! *Ay,* how I missed hearing your voice! *¿Cómo estás?*"

"I'm fine. I told Papá that we're living on a farm. It's actually very nice here."

Frankie ran into the room.

I motioned for Frankie to stand next to me so that we could both put ours ears against the receiver.

"And how's your brother?" Mamá asked.

"Mamá! Mamá! It's me, Frankie. I was in the bathroom and didn't hear the phone ring!"

"Frankie!" Mamá exclaimed. "I didn't know you were on the line. How I love you, my little man! How have you been?"

"Oh, Mamá! It's been—"

I elbowed Frankie and opened my eyes as big as I could. I'd already warned him not to say anything that might make our parents worry.

"It's been . . ." Frankie paused as he thought of what to say next. "Fine," he said, his voice cracking.

"I know this is hard. Just take care of each other

and soon you'll be home." I could hear the quiver in Mamá's own voice. Neither Frankie nor Mamá was fooling anyone.

Frankie opened his mouth to say something, but only a whimper escaped from his lips.

Papá jumped back on the line. "Frankie, *mi hijo*, you're such a brave boy. You've got to be strong so you can protect your sister. Can you do that?"

Frankie nodded.

"Frankie?" Papá asked again.

"He's nodding yes," I said.

"Good. I want you both to think of this as an adventure. You can tell us all the stories when you come back home."

Again, Frankie just nodded.

I closed my eyes, imagining that I was there in my living room. Talking to them face to face. "Do you know when we'll be going home?" I asked.

"No, not yet. Hopefully soon."

Mrs. Baxter touched my shoulder. I knew we had to hang up. We had to limit our time so that we'd have enough money for future calls.

"Papá, we have to go," I said, barely finding my own voice.

"I know, *mi hija*. We'll talk soon. Write to us!"

"We love you!" Mamá and Papá both said.

Frankie and I responded together, too. "*¡Los queremos también!*"

"*¡Adiós!*" they shouted.

"*Adiós,*" we said in unison.

Then we heard a small click and the line went dead.

I slowly hung up the receiver. Frankie ran back to his room. I felt more alone than ever.

Chapter 25

CUBA IS PRESSING TOWARD RED GOAL; REGIME
DIRECTS DRIVE TO SET UP COMMUNIST STATE
—*THE NEW YORK TIMES*, JULY 30, 1961

The warm summer days had become hot summer weeks, but the cool nights were always a reminder that we were far from home. A home that, with each passing day, seemed to drift farther away. I tried to push aside the fear that I might never see my parents again, but the hope that we'd be going back to Cuba, a better Cuba than the one we'd left, was quickly fading.

Every day I'd read the newspaper, searching for more information on Cuba. I was desperate to learn about what was happening back home, but even on days when there was no news about Cuba, I still read all the articles. It kept me up-to-date on what was happening in other parts of the country and the world.

At first, I was surprised that the paper would report

the bad things that happened in the United States and that there were even stories that directly criticized President Kennedy. It was a sharp contrast to Cuba, where anyone who spoke out against the government or Fidel was considered a traitor. I guess the promises made by Castro and Che of helping the less fortunate sounded so good at the time that losing some of your freedoms didn't seem too high a price to pay.

What a difference a few months made! Before, I didn't want to think about people being jailed, killed, or forced to leave their homes. I thought those people must have done something wrong or just didn't love Cuba enough. But now I knew better. It had all become clear. Castro was, in one way or another, eliminating those who did not agree with him. He had even forced my parents to eliminate me from Cuba.

Now I could only hope that my parents would not be eliminated in a more sinister way.

❀   ❀   ❀   ❀   ❀

"We'll only be here five minutes. I just want to say our hellos and leave. I know you want to rush home in case the call to your parents gets connected," Mrs. Baxter said as we walked into the church's social hall.

I nodded. Mrs. Baxter understood the importance of those calls. Usually I loved going to Sunday Mass. That, along with our Tuesday visits to Grand Island to run errands, was the only time we left the farm. But it was more than just leaving the house that made Mass special.

The time we spent in church reminded me of how Cuba used to be, before the priests and nuns were kicked out. The service at St. Mary's was in Latin, just like in Cuba, so for that one hour, I could close my eyes and, with those familiar sounds in my ears, it felt like home.

After Mass, there was always coffee and doughnuts in the parish hall. The Baxters would introduce us to their friends, who were all very pleasant, but none of them had kids our age. The teenagers all seemed to skip the doughnuts and preferred to hang out by the fountain that had a statue of Our Lady of Lourdes in the center. Through the window, I'd see them laughing and having a good time, but I stayed inside with Frankie. I couldn't help wondering if they were sometimes laughing at me.

"Frankie, I spoke with Father Kirkland," Mrs. Baxter said. "He says that once your English is a little better, you can start going to Sunday school with the other kids your age. Won't that be nice? You won't have to stand around here while all us old people catch up with each other."

"I like it here. The doughnuts are good." Frankie leaned over and whispered to me in Spanish, "Does she really think I want more schooling? Maybe I shouldn't learn any more English."

"Don't say that, Frankie," I chided. "Besides, once you know more English, you'll be able to make some friends."

"Nah, I can make friends *without* knowing English. Anyway, it hasn't helped you any."

I stole a glimpse at the girls outside. If any of them wanted to be my friend, wouldn't they approach me?

"Not much to say now, huh?" Frankie teased.

I gave him a shove. I hated that he was right.

"All right, you two, settle down. Frankie, I know how much you love those doughnuts, but today we need to get going. So, hurry up and take one for the road." Mrs. Baxter faced her husband as Frankie rushed to the corner table. "No chitchatting today, Henry. That call from Cuba might come in anytime now."

"Humpf." Mr. Baxter adjusted his jacket. He never seemed comfortable wearing that suit, and by the time we'd reach the car, he usually had the tie undone, and his jacket was ready to be handed over to Mrs. Baxter.

"Helen, Helen!" An older woman with gray hair piled up into a small beehive hairdo called out to Mrs. Baxter.

Mrs. Baxter waved. "Oh, it's Jane. I haven't seen her in months."

"Mmm-hmm." Mr. Baxter pushed his hands deep into his coat pockets.

"Helen, my dear, you look lovely in that blue dress. Makes you look ten years younger." The woman took a sip of her coffee.

"Aw, aren't you sweet? But you've seen this old dress before. If I look younger, it's because of these kids." Mrs. Baxter put her arm around my shoulder and gave it a squeeze. "They're bringing new life into our house."

"Oh yes, I heard that you had some new guests."

Mrs. Baxter grinned. "Yes, this is Lucía. Lucía, this is Mrs. Trenton."

"Nice to meet you." I stretched out my hand.

"Oh, how nice that you speak English." Mrs. Trenton shook my hand. She glanced back at Mrs. Baxter. "She does understand, right?"

Mrs. Baxter nodded.

"Well, it's very nice to finally meet you," Mrs. Trenton continued. "All I heard about when I got back from my trip was the wonderful Cuban children that were staying with the Baxters."

"And that little rascal over there by the doughnuts is Frankie." Mrs. Baxter pointed to the table, where Frankie was balancing a doughnut in his mouth while wrapping another one in a napkin and hiding it in his suit pocket.

"So, it's been going well?" Mrs. Trenton raised an eyebrow, tilting her head toward Mr. Baxter, who was now standing by a few men who looked equally unhappy to be in their suits. "Even with Henry?"

Mrs. Baxter leaned a little closer to Mrs. Trenton and lowered her voice. "Better than I could have imagined. He's taken a real liking to the kids."

I did a double take. Mr. Baxter liking us seemed to

be a bit of an exaggeration. It was more like he tolerated us.

"They are both adorable. If Stan and I were younger, we'd get one, too."

An uncomfortable silence filled the air. I squirmed, remembering how Angela had described us as being like puppies at the pound. Was that how they saw us here?

Mrs. Baxter seemed to be thinking the same thing. "Well, they're not pets, Jane. They're children. Keep that in mind."

"Oh, I didn't mean that the way it sounded. It just seems like such a wonderful thing that you're doing." She gave me an apologetic smile. "All I've done so far is help collect clothing, but I'd like to do more. In fact, I could send over some of the nicer things for Lucía and Frankie."

"That'd be wonderful, Jane. We'll talk again later, but Frankie's done and we need to be going." Mrs. Baxter pointed to Frankie, who was weaving his way back to us with a doughnut in each hand.

"All right. I'll call you," Mrs. Trenton said as Frankie joined us.

I opened my eyes as big as I could at Frankie. Why had he taken so many doughnuts? What would people say? What would Mrs. Trenton think?

"For you and you." He handed one to me and one to Mrs. Baxter.

184

Mrs. Trenton mouthed "So cute" to Mrs. Baxter before walking away.

"Thank you, Frankie. That's very sweet. I'm not very hungry, so you can have mine." Mrs. Baxter smiled as she gave it back to him.

"Okay," he answered, and gobbled it up before she could change her mind.

"*¿Y el que tienes en el bolsillo?*" I pointed to his pocket.

"*Es para* Mr. Baxter," he said, walking over to where the men were standing.

I watched as Frankie tapped Mr. Baxter's arm. All the men stopped talking to look at him. He then pulled out the napkin-wrapped doughnut from his pocket. Mr. Baxter hesitated for a moment, smiled, and patted Frankie on the back.

We were ready to go.

❖   ❖   ❖   ❖   ❖

"Don't worry, Lucía," Mrs. Baxter said as we entered the house. "I'm sure the call didn't come in while we were at church. We were only gone a couple of hours."

"But it's been almost two days since we asked for a line to Cuba." I touched the white phone in the living room, hoping it would ring. Usually, if the call was to be connected at all, it would happen within twenty-four hours.

"Hmm." Mr. Baxter took the Sunday newspaper with him to the back porch.

"Can I go outside and play with my baseball?" Frankie asked.

Mrs. Baxter nodded and placed her small white gloves on the fireplace mantel. "But first, change out of your good clothes. Don't forget to hang the suit back up."

Frankie ran to his room.

The Baxters were good like that. They treated us like we were their own children, which meant we had chores to do, but we were also given freedom to make our own decisions . . . even if they were the wrong ones. Like when Frankie spent his entire weekly allowance on that baseball instead of putting it toward our Calls to Cuba Fund. I couldn't really blame him, though. I secretly wanted to spend some of mine on a lipstick. But I knew how difficult it was for Mamá and Papá to make calls to the U.S., so it was up to us to save all our extra money and call them. But the calls were expensive. We had to space them out to every three or four weeks, and we'd only speak for a couple of minutes. Yet that was our only real expense. I couldn't imagine how my parents were surviving with the little money Papá earned doing odd jobs.

Mrs. Baxter touched my shoulder. "If we don't hear from them today or tomorrow, we'll try again on Tuesday."

I nodded, but I didn't want to wait a few more days. I wanted the call to come in now. It had been almost a month since we'd spoken to Mamá and Papá, and although we'd receive letters from them every few days, I just wanted to hear their voices.

I stared at the phone.

Ring. Please ring.

"Why don't we listen to some music? I'll put on a lovely Andrews Sisters album. That'll get our minds off the waiting." Mrs. Baxter flipped through the record albums that were stored in a dark wooden cabinet.

They reminded me of all the ones I'd left in Cuba. My Elvis, Beny Moré, and Celia Cruz y La Sonora Matancera records. I wondered if they just sat in the corner of my room gathering dust. The music started playing, but it was the song of a different generation, of a different country. I once asked Mrs. Baxter if she had any Ricky Nelson records and she just laughed. Said that was for the young, but if I saved up, I could buy some and she'd let me play them . . . every once in a while.

I twirled the ribbon wrapped around my ponytail as music filled the room. During the last few weeks, the days had been so hot that my hair was almost always picked up. It was no surprise that Mrs. Baxter kept her hair short. She would cut it herself every few weeks and had even offered to trim mine. But I knew how much Mamá loved my long hair, so I'd said no.

If only the phone would ring. I glared at it. *Ring,* I commanded.

The jarring sound of a call coming in startled me. *It worked!*

Mrs. Baxter raced to the phone. "Hello," she said, almost before picking up the receiver.

I waited. Every second was valuable.

"No, Gladys, I can't talk, we're waiting for our call to Cuba." Mrs. Baxter paused. "No, I don't speak to them, the kids do." Another pause.

I pleaded with my eyes for Mrs. Baxter to get off the phone.

"Gladys," Mrs. Baxter continued. "Gladys, I have to hang up. I can't tie up the line. The call could be connected any minute and they'd get a busy signal. No, we never know when the operator will call back with the connection. We'll talk later." Mrs. Baxter hung up the phone and smiled at me. "It was Gladys."

I nodded. Maybe I could do it again. I stared hard at the phone. *Ring. Ring!*

Nothing.

"Why don't you help me prepare a nice Sunday lunch?" Mrs. Baxter held the kitchen door open for me.

I hesitated. It would mean stepping away from the phone.

"I'll turn down the music. We can hear the phone from the kitchen." She walked over to the large piece of furniture that housed the family's record player. Just as the singers were saying "Mr. Sandman, bring me a dream," the phone rang. Mrs. Baxter once again ran toward me and answered the call.

"Yes . . . we placed the call a couple of days ago . . . go ahead. Hello, *un momento*." She smiled and handed me the phone. "Lucía, it's your father. I'll get Frankie."

I was on the clock. I could only afford three minutes and had to leave time for Frankie to talk. I grabbed the phone.

"Papá?"

"*Hola, mi hija.* How are you? How's your brother?"

A sense of joy filled my heart at the sound of his voice.

"*Bien,* Papá. We're both fine. We've been learning a lot of English."

Papá chuckled. "You'll be my little *Americanita* pretty soon. So how's life on a farm?"

I felt my shoulders drop. Just hearing his voice filled me with a sense of calm. Letting me forget for a moment the miles of separation between us. "Good. The corn in some of the fields around here is already higher than my waist, but they say by October it'll be about seven feet high. But tell me I won't see that. That we're going home."

"*Ay, mi hija,* I wish I could." He sighed. "Maybe soon . . . I don't know. Things here are . . ." A clicking noise on the line reminded us both that the soldiers could be listening. Papá's voice became a little stiffer. "Things here are the same. Let's just say people like your *tío* are the ones making all the decisions, but your mother and I are managing."

"But how?" I wrapped the phone cord around my fingers, trying to feel the connection between us.

"We have friends." I could almost hear the smile on his face as he spoke. "And I've been finding jobs painting houses and fixing roofs."

I overheard Mamá say something in the background.

"Yes, yes. Your mother wants me to tell you that she's now taking in some sewing and ironing. She's a working woman! Here, hold on, she wants to speak to you." He paused for a moment. *"Te quiero,* Lucy."

I took a deep breath. I was not going to let Papá know how much my heart was breaking. "I love you, too."

"Lucía, it's Mamá. Your mother. How are you, *mi hija?"*

I smiled. How could I not know it was her? *"Hola,* Mamá. *Estoy bien.* Frankie's doing fine, too. Mrs. Baxter's been teaching us lots of English."

Mrs. Baxter had returned and now beamed at the mention of her name.

Mamá continued talking. "I'm glad you're learning so much, Lucía. You're remembering to use your manners, right?"

"Of course, Mamá. Have you heard from Ivette? I need to talk to her . . . to apologize."

"I know. I think her brigade gets back in August or September. The public schools will start again by then."

"Oh. Well, I sent her a letter, but I'll try again."

"*Mi hija,* remember that all the mail goes through censors, so she might not even get it. Plus, she may not be the same girl who left a few months ago. *Las cosas cambian.*"

"But not everything changes. Anyway, I'm not the same girl, either, but we can still be friends . . . I think."

"What do you mean you're not the same?" Mamá's voice had a worried tone.

"I've just grown up a little. Frankie and I living here, by ourselves, it's different. Not in a bad way, though."

"Lucía, I've seen those Elvis movies where the American teenagers go crazy. *A mi no me gusta eso.* You know I don't approve of that type of thing."

I twisted and untwisted the phone cord. How could Mamá think that movies and TV showed what things were really like?

"I know, Mamá, but things aren't like that here."

"Seriously, I don't want you dating boys, or thinking that just because we're not there, that means . . ."

I shook my head as Mamá kept talking. She was still trying to tell me how to act, even though she was so far away. Yet the last thing I wanted to do with the few seconds we had was argue.

Frankie pulled on my arm. "Hurry up. It's my turn."

I nodded and raised a finger to let him know it would be just one more moment.

"Mamá, I have to go. Don't worry, we haven't even

made any friends. We live on a farm, miles away from the city." I twirled my long ponytail in my hand.

"*Está bien,* but I want you to be happy, too, and make some nice friends. I love you, Lucía, I just worry. Don't wear makeup, either."

I rolled my eyes. "Ugh, *sí,* Mamá."

"And don't wear your skirts too short."

"*Sí,* Mamá."

"And no high heels."

"*Sí,* Mamá. I love you."

I handed the phone to Frankie before she could say anything else.

Mrs. Baxter stood by, looking at her watch. "Fifty seconds," she said.

Frankie started talking about a mile a minute. He wanted to know if they'd received his drawing of the fireworks he'd seen on the Fourth of July. Then he went on to describe every one of them. What a waste of a phone call!

Then again, I couldn't believe Mamá had spent her time with me telling me how to behave. It was like she didn't trust me. She'd sent us to a different country by ourselves, but she was worried about my wearing makeup? Here I was, taking care of Frankie and myself . . . and I was doing a pretty good job. I certainly was old enough to make my own decisions.

"Mrs. Baxter?" I said.

"Frankie, you need to hang up now." Mrs. Baxter touched Frankie's shoulder.

He nodded and said his good-byes.

"Yes, Lucía?" She turned to face me as Frankie rubbed his eyes and hung up the phone.

"I want you to cut my hair . . . short. Really short."

Chapter 26

CUBA EXILES ADJUST TO NEW LIVES
—*ADA EVENING NEWS*, SEPTEMBER 5, 1961

The sun had been up for about an hour, and we'd already gathered the eggs, fed the chickens, had breakfast, and been waiting at the bus stop for over ten minutes. Mrs. Baxter had warned us to leave the house extra early so that we wouldn't miss the bus on the first day of school.

I glanced over at Frankie. He was wearing a pair of dark blue pants that Mrs. Baxter had hemmed for him, with a crisp white shirt and light tan jacket. The only thing slightly off was his penny loafers, which were two sizes too big, but he'd stuffed cotton in the tips so that they wouldn't slip off. He didn't seem to have a care in the world. For him, school was going to be a place to find a few other boys who liked to play catch.

I, on the other hand, wasn't too sure about going to

school. What if people made fun of the way I talked? If I looked strange to them? What if no one spoke to me and I was ignored all day?

Two large headlights shined in the distance.

"You'll be back on the bus after school, right?" Frankie asked.

"Of course."

"And everyone at my school will be my age, right?"

"Yes, more or less. Don't be nervous. Everything is going to be fine. We'll both be fine." I smoothed my hair. It had grown about an inch since I cut it, but it was still just a bit under my chin. I'd flipped the ends and chosen a wide orange headband that matched the checkered dress Mrs. Baxter had fixed for me.

The bus whistled to a stop right in front of us.

This was it. I was about to walk into American teenage life.

Frankie boarded the bus first and said good morning to the driver. I was proud of how quickly he'd learned English during the last few months, although Mrs. Baxter really hadn't given us any option.

When I reached the top of the steps, I noticed that at least one person was sitting in each seat. Frankie and I wouldn't be able to sit together as I'd hoped. I pushed Frankie a little farther down the aisle, past a few teenage boys who had taken over the first two rows. The bus was strangely quiet, and I could feel everyone's eyes on us.

The bus driver closed the door, and Frankie made a beeline for the back, where a boy his age was tossing a baseball. I watched as Frankie told the boy something and then sat down. The two of them started talking. It seemed Frankie had already made a friend.

I took a few steps toward a pretty dark-haired girl who sat toward the middle of the bus on one of the large bench seats. She was whispering something to the redhead in front of her, and both wore dresses somewhat similar to mine. The dark-haired girl even had a headband just like the one I was wearing.

I took a deep breath. At least, I'd made the right choice in selecting which clothes to wear. I smiled at the girl.

She quickly scooted to the aisle side of the seat to let me know that I wasn't going to be sitting next to her.

My heartbeat quickened. Would everyone on the bus act the same way?

I felt a tap on the back of my right arm.

A girl with hair so blond that it looked almost white motioned for me to join her.

I followed her to a seat near the front and quickly sat down, in case the girl changed her mind.

"Hi. I'm Jennifer. You're the girl from Cuba, right?" she asked.

I nodded. Did everyone know about me already?

"I'm Lucía. How do you know I'm from Cuba?"

Jennifer smiled. "In Grand Island, *everyone* knows each other's business. Plus, I got back into town last week after spending the summer at my grandma's in Idaho and I saw you at St. Mary's. The kids there thought you wanted to be left alone, since you never came outside by the fountain and always stayed in the social hall after Mass."

"Oh." I looked down at my notebook.

"Doesn't matter. I figured you were just shy or something. They should've introduced themselves to you anyway."

I felt my shoulders relax a little.

"Are you in ninth grade, too?" I asked.

"Yep. There's about five or six of us farm kids that get picked up to be taken to Central High. Everyone else in here goes to either Grand Island Junior High or Brian Washington Elementary. Hey, do you have your schedule with you? Let's see if we have any classes together." Jennifer took her schedule out and waited while I did the same.

She compared the two while I looked out the window. The rows of green cornstalks had grown to over five feet high, and in the morning breeze they seemed to form ripples, like waves in the ocean. I missed Puerto Mijares. Mamá had told me in her last letter that Ivette was back in town, since classes had started their regular schedule in Cuba, too. I'd already written Ivette several times, asking her to forgive me, but she hadn't replied.

"We have first period, which will also be our homeroom, plus lunch and two more classes together. It's perfect 'cause, you know, it's all new for me, too. Not the people, but going to high school. We can walk in together, 'cause you know what they call us freshmen?" Jennifer's blue eyes twinkled. "Fresh meat."

I smiled. I liked this girl.

"Holy moly!" Jennifer was still reading my schedule. "You've got Honors Algebra II with Mrs. Armistedge. I heard from my older brother that she's super tough. You must have done really well on your placement test."

I shrugged. I'd learned a lot back in Señora Cardoza's algebra class, and in math you didn't need to know much English. It was strange. Part of me felt like it was only yesterday that I was sitting in my classes in Cuba, but at the same time, it seemed like a lifetime ago.

"You see her over there?" Jennifer pointed to a girl with silver-tipped glasses sitting a few rows behind us. "She's super smart in math, too. She'll probably be in that class with you. Her name is Doris and she's really nice."

The girl had her face buried in a book.

"Doris!" Jennifer waved at the girl as the bus stopped again.

Doris looked up, gave us both a slight wave, then went back to her reading.

Suddenly I felt someone tickle me under my ribs. "Hey, guess who!" a deep voice said.

I spun around to see a tall boy with beautiful greased-back brown hair.

"Oh!" He jumped back. "I thought you were someone else."

The dark-haired girl who wouldn't let me sit with her started to laugh.

"Charlie, did you think that was me?" she called out, patting the seat to have this boy join her.

He tossed up his hands. "Sorry, Betty, from behind she kinda looks like you."

"You are so silly!" I watched as she put her arms around his neck and gave him a hug. "I guess you got confused because she's wearing one of my old dresses. You know, the ones I give to the needy." She then looked straight at me and flashed a fake smile. "Isn't it cute that they gave it to her to wear on the first day of high school?"

Suddenly I hated what I was wearing. I wanted to tear it off my body. I wished the ground would open up and swallow me so that I could disappear.

"Don't worry about her. She thinks she's God's gift to Grand Island, but it's all in her head." Jennifer smiled and gave me a nudge. "It's pretty much the only thing that's in there . . . she's as dumb as they come."

I turned around and faced forward. I'd been on the bus for about five minutes and already I knew who my friends and enemies were going to be.

❁　❁　❁　❁　❁

All around me, people were shouting hellos, and girls squealed at the sight of each other. It was the official start of school. As the crowd swarmed past me, I stopped to take in my surroundings. The building didn't look so big when I'd come in to register and take my placement test, but now that it was filled with students, I felt as if I were just a speck. A speck no one seemed to notice, which was fine with me.

The green-painted hallways were all lined with lockers, and above each classroom door hung a bronze plate showing the room number. At the end of the corridor was an expansive stairway that led to the second floor. Jennifer had already warned me not to fall for the prank of being told that the pool was on the third floor. There was no pool or third floor. In fact, since I was a freshman, all my classes would be on the first floor, making it easier for me to find my way around.

"C'mon." Jennifer pulled me by the arm. "Our class is over here. Room 122."

We entered a half-empty classroom and headed straight for the back. I quickly put my notebook on the desk next to Jennifer's. There was still about a minute before the bell would ring and the teacher was busy writing the day's lesson on the chalkboard.

Unfortunately, my first class was going to be the subject I dreaded most . . . English. I wished the day would have started with something else, like math or science. Even PE would have been better.

As the bell rang, kids ran into the room and sat in the remaining chairs.

The teacher turned to face us. She was a middle-aged woman who looked rather ordinary except for the large mole on her left cheek. She wore a dark blue dress and her hair was neatly piled on top of her head. "All right, class, settle down. I'm Mrs. Brolin and I'll be your English teacher this year."

A chime sounded over the loudspeaker, interrupting the classroom chatter.

"Good morning, students," a voice announced. "This is your principal, Mr. Pikowski. I expect all of you had an enjoyable summer and are eager to begin the school year. As is tradition, starting tomorrow, your senior-class president, Melissa Powers, will give the daily announcements. But for today, I want to extend a warm welcome . . ."

I froze. *Oh no. Don't mention me.*

". . . to our newest students . . ."

No, please no.

". . . our incoming freshman class."

I let out the breath I'd been holding.

Mr. Pikowski continued, "Some of you are coming to us from Grand Island Junior High, others are from

Oakes Academy, but now we are all Central High Falcons. I do want to remind all of you that as you make new friends and share new experiences, that *you* are the leaders of tomorrow. We hope you enjoy your four years here, and after you graduate, may you go out into the world to make us proud. Have a wonderful first day of school."

Jennifer rolled her eyes.

I smiled. I was already "out in the world," and I'd been trying my best to make my parents proud. I glanced at everyone around me. They weren't that different from the kids in Cuba. A little more pale, and there were a few more blonds in the class, but generally the same. It seemed like I might be able to blend in, at least for a little while.

Mrs. Brolin began taking attendance and had already called out three or four names when she got to me.

"Miss Lucía Álvarez?" she said.

"Present," I answered in perfect English. I'd practiced so that there wouldn't be a trace of a Cuban accent.

Mrs. Brolin paused and walked down the aisle toward me.

What was she doing?

She placed a hand on my shoulder. "Class, I want you all to take notice of Miss Álvarez . . ."

Everyone turned in their seats to stare at me.

". . . and help her adjust to life in Nebraska. She's from Cuba, and I'm sure you have all read in the newspapers about the situation there. If she needs help, I expect all of you to step in and assist her." Mrs. Brolin patted my shoulder and strutted back to her desk.

She was acting all proud of herself. Didn't she realize that being singled out was the very last thing I wanted?

I sank down in my seat, praying that everyone would go back to whatever they were doing before.

To my amazement, most of them did. Everyone except a tall boy with freckles who sat closer to the front. He smiled and gave me a little wave.

My reaction was to quickly look down at my notebook.

When I glanced back, he held up a piece of notebook paper that said, "Hi, I'm Eddie."

I gave him a nod.

I was pretty sure that this was not the attention that Mrs. Brolin intended.

Mrs. Baxter took a strawberry and sat on my bed. "So, how goes it? Are you feeling a bit overwhelmed by the schoolwork?"

"No. Why? Did Frankie say something?"

"Oh, goodness no. I just know that starting high school can be a difficult transition for any young girl. I can only imagine how much harder it is under your circumstances." She took a bite of the berry, waiting for me to respond.

Math would have to wait for a few minutes. I put down my pencil. "I guess school is a little hard."

"Mmm-hmm." She nodded.

I shrugged. "Trying to keep up with everything that the teachers say in English and take notes at the same time, it makes my brain hurt sometimes."

Mrs. Baxter chuckled. "Oh, we all have days like that. I remember when I started secretarial school, how much pressure I put on myself. I was the first in my family to go past high school, and, well, I would've loved to have gone to college and been a teacher, but I wasn't smart enough for that. So, I *had* to do well in secretarial school."

"And did you?" I asked, reaching for one of the strawberries.

"Of course. But those first few weeks were real doozies. Late nights studying and worrying. Then I found a sort of rhythm and began to enjoy myself. You will, too." She patted my knee. "You'll see."

"I hope so. I just want to get good grades, because Papá always said that what's in here"—I tapped my head—"no one can take from you."

"Your father is a very wise man."

"Yes, he is." My shoulders relaxed and seemed to drop a couple of inches. It felt good to talk things over with Mrs. Baxter.

"I'll let you get back to your studying, but I have one thing to add to what your father said. I think they can't take what's here"—she touched her forehead—"or here." She placed a hand over her heart.

I smiled. Next to my parents, Mrs. Baxter was the smartest person I knew.

Chapter 28

FIRING SQUADS HAVE ONLY STARTED,
DECLARES CASTRO
—*THE YUMA DAILY SUN*, SEPTEMBER 29, 1961

In less than a month, crossing the Nebraska plains in the yellow school bus and going to school in Grand Island had become a familiar routine. Every morning, I'd sit with Jennifer in the fifth row of the bus and Frankie would head to the back with his friends. Most of the students had gone out of their way to be nice and help me if I didn't understand something. Most . . . but not all. There were a few who were not happy with the attention I sometimes got.

"Did Alex Murphy just say hi to you?" Jennifer asked, waiting by her locker.

I giggled. "Uh-huh."

Jennifer bounced up and down. "You see. Even the cute varsity football players know who you are. You are so lucky. Next year, when we get to date, you're going to have your pick of guys."

"Ooh, this sounds like an interesting conversation. Does someone here have a crush?" Betty stepped from behind the library door, which was just a few feet from Jennifer's locker.

"Why don't you go and take your Betty-ites with you." Jennifer pointed to the trio of girls who always followed Betty wherever she went.

"Jenny, dear, when are you going to learn that no one listens to you?" Betty cocked her head and flashed me a smile. "So, you *really* think that just because a boy says hello to you, he actually may like you?"

I stayed quiet. I wanted to have a smart comeback, but by the time I thought of something in English, most conversations had usually moved on.

"Look, girls, she's blushing. Isn't that cute?" Betty glanced around as the trio started giggling.

The first bell rang, letting everyone know that classes would start in two minutes.

"Don't be such a jerk, Betty. Just leave us alone." Jennifer slammed her locker door.

It had taken me a while to think of something to say, but I couldn't be a doormat. "Jealous?" I asked, flicking my hair back as we walked past Betty on our way to homeroom.

"Of what? A little tamale like you?" Betty called out. "You're just a pet project for the people around here.

A sharp pain sliced through my heart. Mamá and Papá had never seen snow. I wondered if they ever would.

I followed Frankie's lead and looked up at the falling snow. It felt like soft kisses from heaven landing on my nose and forehead. Almost as if someone were trying to tell me not to be sad. That everything would be all right.

Frankie twirled around and around. "This is great! What a birthday!" he shouted.

As we walked down the small road toward the Baxter farm, the ground started to turn white. By the time we got to the Baxters' front porch, a thin layer of snow had covered the top railing. Frankie ran his hand over the long piece of wood and quickly flicked a bit of snow toward me.

The white powder scattered against my coat. I dropped my books on the floor of the porch and chased Frankie out into the field. For the next hour, I ran around like a little kid. Swiping at the flurries as the wind blew stronger. And the harder it snowed, the better Frankie and I liked it.

"It's almost five. You two snow-loving kids need to come inside and get ready for dinner. We have a birthday to celebrate," Mrs. Baxter yelled from the front door.

We ran inside, shaking the ice crystals off our clothes.

"Gee whiz, is it always like that?" Frankie tossed aside his scarf while he hung up his coat.

"*Ahem.* Frankie . . ." Mrs. Baxter pointed to the scarf.

"Yes, ma'am." He picked it up and draped it over the large hook.

Mrs. Baxter smiled. "Just wait till tonight. You haven't seen anything yet!"

"I'm gonna watch it some more!" Frankie ran toward the large picture window.

"Should I go ahead and set the table?" I asked.

"Sure, but Mr. Baxter isn't home yet. It's a good thing we're celebrating your birthday, with the kinda day he's had." She opened the bottom drawer of the china cabinet. "He has a soft spot for you kids, you know?"

"Soft spot? I don't understand."

Mrs. Baxter took something out of the drawer and held it behind her back as she turned around to face me. "It means he has a warm place in his heart."

I was confused. "His heart is warm? Is that why he went to the doctor today?"

She laughed. "No, no. The doctor told him his back needs more time to heal. It'll be another couple of months before he can farm again, but his heart is fine. What I meant to say is that he likes having you and Frankie around." She gave me a wink. "Keeps his mind off his injury."

"Oh." Even though Mr. Baxter never said much, he'd started to toss a ball around with Frankie every night after dinner. He also drove me to Jennifer's house on Saturdays when he went to work. Maybe he did like us.

"I have something for you." Mrs. Baxter held a small black box tied with a thin pink ribbon. "It's not much. I used to wear it when I was your age. But since I never had a daughter . . . well, I just thought you might like to have it."

I opened the box. Inside was a gold chain with a small cross. It reminded me of my silver necklace back in Cuba.

"Do you like it?" she asked.

I could barely get the words out. "It's beautiful. I love it." I gave Mrs. Baxter a big hug. "Thank you."

She turned me around and draped the necklace in front of me. As she fastened the clasp in the back, she whispered, "You're a very special girl, Lucía Álvarez. I'm very glad you came into our lives."

My chest tightened. I couldn't breathe. Feelings of sadness and joy overwhelmed me. I missed Mamá and Papá so much, yet the Baxters were such kind people that I couldn't be completely unhappy. On a day when I should have been miserable, I actually wanted to laugh.

Mrs. Baxter rubbed my arms. "I think I hear

Mr. Baxter's car. You and Frankie go wash up. I made your favorites tonight."

I looked back at her. "You mean . . . ?"

She smiled. "Mmm-hmm. Cheeseburgers, french fries, and chocolate cake for dessert!"

❊   ❊   ❊   ❊   ❊

"This is for you, Lucy. I did it myself." Frankie reached under the table and gave me a frame made out of Popsicle sticks. "You can put that picture of Mamá and Papá with us at the beach in it."

"Mail came." Mr. Baxter placed an envelope next to my dinner plate.

Immediately I knew it was a birthday card from my parents.

"Read it," Frankie said, passing the french fries.

I opened Mamá and Papá's card. It showed a beautiful girl holding a bouquet of flowers, with the words *"Feliz Cumpleaños"* written in silver letters. I showed everyone at the table.

Inside, Mamá wrote about how she missed me. About how on the day I was born, she realized that the only thing she'd ever wanted to be was my mother. She said that Frankie and I were her most prized possessions, and knowing that we were safe was the only way she could survive being apart from me on my fifteenth birthday.

I took a deep breath.

Papá simply wrote that he loved me very much. He

said that Mamá had made the card sappy enough and that he hoped I was happy celebrating my day. That hopefully we would be together soon.

I smiled. It was typical of Papá to try to get me into a better mood . . . even from far away.

Frankie took a bite of his cheeseburger. Ketchup squirted out the sides and onto his cheek. "Nothing for me, huh?"

"What did you expect? It's *my* birthday. Oh, wait, it says here that they send their love to my annoying little brother."

"Ha, ha. Very funny."

Mr. Baxter wiped his mouth with his napkin. "Guess everyone gave you their presents."

I touched the little gold cross. I hoped he wasn't upset that I'd been given such a nice gift. I could always give it back.

" 'Cept me." He glanced out the window. "Thought if the weather clears up this weekend, I'd teach you how to drive . . . if you want."

I wasn't sure I understood correctly. Even Mamá didn't know how to drive. She never thought it was necessary. "A car?" I asked.

Mr. Baxter nodded. "You're fifteen. You can get a learner's permit."

I couldn't believe it. I, Lucía Álvarez, was actually going to learn how to drive!

I jumped up and gave him a hug.

"Oh . . ." He patted me on the shoulder. "Well, yes, that'll do."

I stepped back and smiled. This hadn't been such a horrible day after all.

＊　＊　＊　＊　＊

The glow from my desk light created a funny shadow against the room's wood paneling. I stared at the blank piece of paper in front of me. I didn't know how to start my letter to my parents. Should I mention the gifts the Baxters gave me? Would that make them happy or sad?

"Um, Lucía."

I looked up to see Mr. Baxter standing in my doorway. "Yes, sir?"

He took a step in and held out an envelope. "This got mixed in with some of the bills. It's for you. From Cuba."

Immediately I reached out for it and noticed it had no return address. Yet I knew the handwriting. It was from Ivette. "It's from my best friend in Cuba!"

"Hmm." Mr. Baxter nodded as he turned to go back down the hall.

The familiar handwriting brought back memories of all the notes we used to pass each other in class. Now our notes would have to travel much farther. I sat on the bed and opened the envelope.

> Dear Lucy,
>   I saw your mother the other day and she told me that you'd written me several letters

to apologize for how things had ended between us. I want you to know that I never received any of your letters, but of course I forgive you for everything. I'm figuring that my parents threw the letters away because they think you might be a bad influence on me. I don't care what they think. We are still best friends, right? Who else will travel to Paris with me to see all the fashion houses someday?

I nodded as if she could see me answer her.

But just so I can get your letters, send them to your house, and I'll come up with an excuse to pass by and see your parents. I'll only be able to do this every once in a while because, now that your parents have requested exit visas, they're always being watched.

My heart leapt into my throat. My parents had asked to leave Cuba? Why hadn't they told me? I knew exit visas could take months, and sometimes years, to be approved, but why not say something? Did this mean there was no chance of my going home? My hands trembled as I read more of Ivette's letter, but the next couple of paragraphs only talked about the latest school gossip and how the *brigadista* uniform was now considered all the rage. But then her tone got serious.

Lucy, something happened to me this summer that I haven't been able to tell anyone. I can't keep it inside any longer, but you have to promise not to tell and to never, ever bring it up again. Do you promise?

I silently made the promise.

I'm not even sure how to write about it. See, while I was working with the brigades in one of the mountain villages, I met this really cute soldier. I won't even tell you his name because that's not important. We started talking every day and he'd sit with me and wait for my bus. One evening, he asked if he could walk me back to where I was living instead of my taking the bus. He said that way we could talk a little more. Lucy, he didn't want to just talk or kiss, he wanted much more.

I gasped. If only I'd been there for her, to help her. I was almost afraid to keep reading. I took a deep breath and looked back at her letter.

I screamed when he grabbed at me, but no one seemed to hear. I'm not sure if in the end he was too strong for me or if I was just too scared to fight back. It was the worst night of my life, and afterward he never even spoke to me again.

My stomach churned. This was much worse than I imagined. I hated the soldiers! All of them!

Please, please don't say anything. Not even to me. And don't blame the brigades or the revolution. I was just, well, I was just unlucky.

Unlucky? This didn't sound like Ivette. Where was her anger? Her thoughts about payback and getting even. That soldier was scum and something should be done about it.

How about you? I hope you haven't been caught in any race riots. I read that they are happening everywhere and how everything is so dangerous in the United States. There are so many awful, violent people living there, I don't know how you are surviving. But don't worry, soon your parents will realize that things are better here, and they'll forget about leaving and bring you back. You'll finally escape that nightmare.

I sighed. After seeing both countries firsthand, it seemed like Ivette was the one who needed to survive. She signed the letter:

Besos, Ivette

But it was the three words, written in large letters at the very bottom of the page, that sent a chill down my spine. It simply said . . .

¡Viva La Revolución!

Chapter 30

CASTRO AGAIN TELLS ABOUT
KEEPING RED VIEWS SECRET
—*THE FRESNO BEE REPUBLICAN*, DECEMBER 24, 1961

The Baxter house sparkled with multicolored lights and evergreen garlands draped with icicles. The piney scent of a real Christmas tree mixed with the aroma of cinnamon from the gingerbread cookies reminded me of . . . nothing. Christmas Eve was not like this in Cuba.

Here, everyone talked about Santa Claus bringing presents the next morning, and Mrs. Baxter planned on making a ham, scalloped potatoes, and her special carrot-pineapple gelatin salad for our Christmas Day lunch. But Christmas Eve was like any other day during the holiday season.

For me, *Nochebuena* meant the smell of onions and garlic cooking while my parents prepared the roasted pig, *el lechón*. We'd also have black beans, rice, and yuca. There'd be music playing, and those rhythmic sounds would get inside me and make me want to dance the whole day. It was wonderful how everyone, Tío Antonio, Abuela (before she died), and even some of our neighbors would come over and have dinner with us. I didn't have a big family like Ivette, but on Christmas Eve, you'd never guess that. Tables would be set up outside where we'd eat, laugh, and play dominoes under the stars until it was time to go to midnight Mass. It was like one big party.

I bit the edge of the letter I'd just written to Ivette. If only she'd see what it was really like here, she wouldn't mistrust the Americans so much. I wanted her to see all the similarities, but in the end, there was no comparison. As much as I liked being in the U.S., Cuba was my home.

"Lucía, can you go get Frankie? Mr. Baxter is washing up already." Mrs. Baxter placed two trivets on the dining room table.

"I'm here. Hope dinner is ready 'cause I'm as hungry as a house." Frankie bounded toward the table.

"You mean hungry as a horse," Mrs. Baxter corrected him.

"Ohhh. Now it makes sense." Frankie started pouring water into each person's glass.

"Ready, Helen?" Mr. Baxter asked, walking to the table and taking his seat.

"Yes, one second." She made a quick run to the kitchen and brought out a covered dish.

"We can help you, Mrs. Baxter," I said, prodding Frankie to stand up.

"No, no, not today. I want you all to stay seated." She ran back three more times, bringing out more covered dishes.

When everything was out, she looked at Mr. Baxter and said, "Now we're ready."

Mr. Baxter nodded. "Thank you, Lord, for this food we're about to receive. Thank you for our many blessings. Keep us and our families, both those in Boston and Cuba, safe from harm. Amen."

I smiled as we all said "Amen." Mr. Baxter always said grace before dinner, but it was during the last couple of weeks that he'd started mentioning not only Carl but also my parents. It was like we were all somehow related.

Frankie reached over to uncover the dish closest to him, but Mrs. Baxter put a hand over it.

"Hold on, Frankie. I want to say something."

Mr. Baxter leaned back in his chair.

"I know it's been difficult for the two of you to be away from home and all your customs during the holidays. I didn't even know that you celebrated Christmas Eve instead of Christmas Day until Lucía mentioned it a couple of days ago. Anyway, I did the best I could with the food. Had to improvise a little, though."

Mrs. Baxter uncovered the first two dishes. Rather than our typical roasted pig and black beans, Mrs. Baxter had made pork chops and baked beans.

I smiled from ear to ear.

"This one was easy." She uncovered a bowl of white rice. "But I had no idea what yuca was, so I made"—she removed the final lid—"potatoes."

"I never liked yuca anyway," Frankie said, already holding his plate up to be served.

"Thank you," I said softly.

Mrs. Baxter grinned. "And tonight we all have to go to bed early because Santa Claus will be visiting."

"Wait, if Santa Claus brings us toys on Christmas, do *los tres reyes magos* still bring us stuff on January sixth?" Frankie asked.

"No, Frankie." I shook my head. "I already told you. The three wise men bring toys on January sixth to children who live in Cuba. If you live in the U.S., Santa Claus might bring you something on December twenty-fifth. You don't get both. Isn't that right, Mrs. Baxter?"

"Afraid so, Frankie. But think of it this way, you'll get to play with your toys all the sooner."

"Oh, I don't mind. Just as long as someone knows I'm here."

Mrs. Baxter looked over at her husband with a secretive smile. "I wouldn't worry, Frankie," she said. "I think someone knows."

Chapter 31

CASTRO PLEDGES FIGHT TO DEATH
—*THE HUMBOLDT STANDARD*, DECEMBER 25, 1961

In my dream, television star Ricky Nelson was lying by me on a beach in Varadero while Jennifer and Ivette tossed a Frisbee along the water's edge. The air was full of the ocean's saltiness, and I could feel the warmth of the sun on my bare legs. It was as perfect a day as I could imagine, and I didn't want to leave it behind.

"Wake up! C'mon, wake up!" Frankie shook me by the shoulder.

I buried my head beneath the pillow.

"Lucy, it's Christmas. There are presents under the tree. I already peeked and saw them. Hurry!" He pulled my arm, almost dragging me off the bed.

"All right, all right. I'm up." I wiped the sleep out of my eyes, put on my robe, and followed Frankie back to the living room.

"Merry Christmas!" Mrs. Baxter greeted both of us with a hug while Mr. Baxter set up his home-movie camera to film us opening our gifts. "Go ahead, you two. Check your stockings. See if Santa brought you anything." She glanced back at Mr. Baxter. "You got that thing working, Henry?"

"Humpf. All full of dust," Mr. Baxter muttered, blowing into the lens.

I walked to the red stocking that hung on the fireplace. Frankie had already slipped his stocking off its hook and was sticking his hand down into it.

"Well? What did Santa bring you, Frankie?" Mrs. Baxter asked.

"Woo-hoo!" Frankie yelled without fully pulling out his gift. "I know what this is!" He wiggled a baseball glove out from the stocking. "Wow!" Frankie stared at the brown leather mitt. "It's a real Mickey Mantle glove! Look, Mr. Baxter!" Frankie ran over to show the camera and Mr. Baxter. "It's a perfect fit," he said, putting on the glove.

"And you, Lucía?" Mrs. Baxter smiled, her hands clasped together.

I reached down into the stocking and pulled out a small silver compact of pressed powder and a tube of pink lipstick.

A huge smile spread across my face. I was finally going to start wearing some makeup. I felt like whooping and hollering, too.

"Thank you," I said.

Mr. Baxter gave me a slight nod from behind the camera.

"Oh, we didn't have anything to do with those gifts. Those were from Santa Claus. Our gifts are here." Mrs. Baxter pulled out three boxes from beneath the tree.

"More presents!" Frankie shouted, removing the glove.

"These are a little more practical, though. We can't be as extravagant as Santa." Mrs. Baxter waved at the camera and then handed Frankie a box.

Frankie quickly ripped the wrapping and opened his gift. He pulled out a plaid shirt, two pairs of socks, and a new baseball. "Cool," he declared, dropping the clothes on the floor and grabbing the ball to try it out with his glove.

By this time, I was opening my own box. The Baxters had given me a new checkered skirt, a bright pink sweater, and a knitted scarf.

"I hope it all fits," Mrs. Baxter said.

I draped the skirt around my waist. "I'm sure it does. I'll wear it to Mass today! I love it all."

Mrs. Baxter smiled. "I knitted that scarf myself, you know."

I wrapped it around my neck, flinging one end over my shoulder as if I were a movie star. "In that case, I love it even more!"

I'd sewn in home economics class and the Popsicle ornaments and drawings Frankie had made.

"What are you doing?" Frankie tossed his baseball in and out of the glove.

"Nothing." I looked outside. There was no sign of the mailman. Normally, he came at two. He was already more than an hour late. "You know, you should practice your Spanish with me. Nowadays, you're always speaking to me in English. You'd better not forget who you are," I said.

"Your mouth looks weird," he answered me in English, ignoring my comment about his Spanish.

"What? No, it doesn't. *Tú eres* weird," I said as he walked back up the stairs to his room.

As soon as he left, I got up to check myself in the small bathroom under the stairs. I gazed at my image in the mirror from different angles. In the last few months, my body had changed and I had more curves. I puckered my bright pink lips. He's just not used to seeing me with makeup. All the girls at school wore a little bit of makeup, so it had felt strange not wearing any. Now I'd be more like a normal American teenage girl, except for my accent, but that was something Jennifer insisted was part of what made me unique and more interesting.

I heard the front door open. I poked my head out into the hallway and saw Mr. Baxter hanging up his coat.

"My, you're home early. It's not even four!" Mrs. Baxter gave him a kiss on the cheek.

"Humpf." Mr. Baxter took off his hat. "It was slow and the store closed early."

"No wonder. Who wants to go out in this nasty cold weather? Forecasters say it's dipping below zero tonight, but it'll be back in the twenties in a couple of days."

I glanced over at the silent phone.

"Lucía"—Mr. Baxter held out an envelope—"this came."

"Is that what I think it is?" Mrs. Baxter said.

I looked at the postage. "It's from Cuba!" I saw there was no return address. It was from Ivette. After her letter to me, I'd written her back describing how life in the U.S. was different, but nice. I'd told her all about the Baxters and Jennifer. I'd even told her how things in this country were nothing like she thought. How people were helpful, and that it felt great to know that I could speak my mind without fear that someone in the government might not approve. For two months, I hadn't heard from her, until now.

I tore open the envelope.

Dear Lucía,

Happy New Year! I'm mailing this letter way in advance in the hope that it gets to you sometime close to January first. How have you been? Here in Cuba, everything is going great. I've become more involved with the brigades and feel so lucky to be able to help the revolution. I've enrolled so many new students, and now I realize that devoting myself to the revolution is what I was meant to do.

I shook my head. This didn't sound like the Ivette that I knew.

> After reading your last letter, I worry so much about you living in that capitalist society. You probably still think about silly things like the latest fashions or what the newest rock 'n' roll song is. I wish you were here so you could learn to appreciate the goals and ideals Castro has for our country. Hopefully, you've come to your senses and realized that you can't trust the Americans. I don't want to be mean, because I know you must be lonely over there, but I don't want you to get fooled into thinking that just because they pretend to treat you well, they are actually your friends. They're not. We here in Cuba are your true friends. Your comrades. I hope you come home soon before it's too late.

I took a deep breath and slowly exhaled. How could I explain to Ivette that she was completely wrong about . . . well, about everything? I continued reading.

Maybe now, after your father's accident, your parents will send for you.

Accident? My heart started to race. A huge lump formed in my throat and a small moan escaped from my lips.

"Everything okay, Lucía?" Mrs. Baxter asked.

I didn't answer. Instead, all my energy was focused on the letter.

I really couldn't believe it when I heard he'd fallen off a ladder while working on Captain García's roof. Please let me know how he's doing. Since he got transferred to the hospital in Holguín, I haven't heard anything else about him.

I thought back to all my letters where I asked Papá to be careful. I knew that people who didn't support the revolution sometimes met with so-called accidents. Could someone have tried to hurt Papá on purpose? It was almost too much to take in. A shaking started from deep inside my body. My knees began to quiver.

The rest of the letter just talked about what else Ivette was doing and what her life was like with the brigades. I couldn't focus on any of those things. I had to get in touch with Mamá. I stuffed the letter into my skirt pocket.

"Lucía, something's wrong. What is it?" Mrs. Baxter put her arm around me.

"It's my father. He's been hurt. I have to talk to Mamá. I have to!"

"I'll call." Mr. Baxter picked up the phone and took out the handwritten instructions on how to make an international call to Cuba.

Frankie walked into the room, still tossing the ball. "What's going on?"

"No, wait," I said. "She's not home." I turned toward Frankie. "Papá had an accident. He was taken to a hospital in Holguín." A tear streaked down my face as I looked at Mr. Baxter. "It must be bad if they had to take him there."

"I'll contact Father Kirkland at St. Mary's. He can make some calls and try to get us the hospital's number."

❊   ❊   ❊   ❊   ❊

That night, all four of us sat together and prayed the rosary. Before going to bed, Mr. Baxter insisted on placing another call to my house in Cuba . . . just in case.

It was about eleven-thirty when the phone rang.

Mrs. Baxter ran out of her room, curlers in her hair, wearing a light blue velour robe. I met her by the phone in my own flannel pajamas just as she picked up the receiver. Apparently, neither one of us had been able to go to sleep.

"Hello?" She looked at me and nodded. "Yes, operator, please connect us." She thrust the phone toward me as Mr. Baxter rushed in, still struggling to put on his robe.

"Mamá?" I said.

"*¿Lucía? Ay, mi hija. ¡Cómo te extraño!*"

"I miss you, too, Mamá. How's Papá? Ivette told me there was an accident. Why didn't you tell me?"

"*Sí, mi hija.* It happened a couple of weeks ago. Didn't you get my letters?"

"No, what letters? And how's Papá?" I braced myself in case the news was really bad.

Mr. and Mrs. Baxter stared at me, not understanding anything I was saying.

"I sent you letters from the hospital telling you everything, and how he was doing better. I'm sure I sent them to the correct address."

"I never got them. But, Mamá, *díme la verdad*, is Papá okay?"

"*Sí, sí.* He was at the top of a ladder when it tipped over. But don't worry. *No fue nada.*"

My heart pounded inside my throat. "It was nothing? How can you say that? You're not telling me everything. They don't transfer people to the hospital in Holguín for no reason." I inhaled slowly, trying to stay calm. "Mamá, I'm not a little girl, tell me the truth."

"You're right," she sighed, "you're not a little girl anymore."

240

Neither of us spoke for a moment.

"He cracked a few ribs and shattered his right leg."

My hands trembled. "Uh-huh." I knew there was more she wasn't saying.

"And he was unconscious for a few days," she said in a soft voice.

"*¿EN COMA?*"

Mr. Baxter put his hand on my shoulder, and Mrs. Baxter began to cry.

"No, no. He already woke up. He's been at the hospital because he punctured one of his lungs, and they may have to operate on his leg again when the swelling goes down. I just came home today to pick up some clothes, and I'll take the bus back there tomorrow. I'm staying with an old friend of mine in Holguín."

I looked at the Baxters' worried faces. "He's okay," I whispered.

A sense of relief crossed their faces. Mrs. Baxter went to sit on the living room couch while Mr. Baxter stood next to me.

"Mamá, I can't talk much longer, but give me the address and phone number of where you're staying."

I wrote down the information she gave me.

"*¿Y tu hermano?* Does he know about your father?"

"*Sí.* Frankie knows. He's okay, but he's sleeping."

"Wait!" Mrs. Baxter sprang off the couch. She raced to Frankie's room.

"Mamá, I think Mrs. Baxter went to get him."

"I love you, Lucía. Your father does, too."

I smiled. It felt like a boulder had been lifted off my chest. "I love you, too."

"Don't do any crazy things."

I touched my short hair. "Yes, Mamá."

"Behave like a proper young lady."

I squeezed the twisted phone cord and thought of my new lipstick. "*Sí,* Mamá."

Frankie rushed into the room, still wiping the sleep from his eyes.

"Frankie's here. Give Papá a kiss for me. Hopefully, we'll be together soon."

"Love you, Lucía. *¡Feliz año nuevo!*"

"Happy New Year to you, too."

I handed Frankie the phone and thought about this new year. Would it really be all that happy?

Chapter 33

CASTRO DENOUNCES U.S., ROARS DEFIANCE OF OAS
—*THE TIMES RECORD*, FEBRUARY 5, 1962

High school, I had come to realize, did not revolve around the usual four seasons on the calendar. Instead, it was divided into football, basketball, and baseball seasons. It being February, we were in the middle of basketball season.

"My mom can swing by your house at around five-thirty to take us to the game. Is that good for you?" Jennifer asked.

I twirled the twisted phone cord in one hand. "Mmm-hmm. Guess so," I answered, cradling the receiver between my ear and shoulder. I really wasn't in the mood to do much of anything at that moment. Just before Jennifer called, I'd been rereading one of Papá's recent letters. In it he had described how happy he was to finally be leaving the hospital after undergoing his third and, hopefully, final surgery, but he also mentioned how it pained him to go back home. He said Cuba was a changed place, one that I would no longer recognize, nor want to see. A sadness seeped through his words and made its way straight into my heart.

Yet I couldn't help thinking how wrong he was. I still wanted to see Cuba, no matter what it was like. As much as I appreciated everything the Baxters, Jennifer, and the U.S. did for me and Frankie, I missed my home.

"You don't sound too happy about going tonight. Did Eddie say something again? I thought he got the message that you weren't really interested in him."

"No." I untangled the phone cord. "I was just missing being home. And as for Eddie, I don't know anymore. He *is* nice."

"Wait. Are you saying what I think you're saying? That you like Eddie? The boy who has had a crush on you from the first day of school, and who you've basically ignored all this time?" I could hear the excitement in Jennifer's voice.

I started to blush. "He's just so sweet and funny."

"Uh-huh . . . a-a-a-and?"

"And nothing. Eddie and I are just friends. Plus, neither you or I can date until we're sixteen, remember?"

"But would you date him in November?"

"I don't know." I giggled.

"Ooh, this is so good!" she squealed. "Does Eddie suspect that you like him?"

"NO! I'm not sure what I feel. Besides, I'd die if he found out, so don't say anything."

Jennifer laughed. "You know I wouldn't. But how great it would be if you and I could double-date next year! You with Eddie, and me with Nathan. They're best friends and we're best friends!"

"I thought you said Nathan Dixon was a moron?"

"But he's a very cute moron!"

I laughed. Jennifer had a way of always making me feel better.

As soon as I hung up the phone, Frankie appeared from around the corner.

I crossed my arms and gave him my best stare-down face. "Were you eavesdropping?"

"Me? I wouldn't do that." He sauntered around me like a cat ready to pounce.

"Frankie?"

"What? You think I might say something about you . . . being in lo-o-o-ove?"

"Frankie!" I reached out to grab him, but he laughed, stepping aside while making smooching noises.

He started running through the house. "Lucía and Eddie, sitting in a tree. K-I-S-S-I—"

"STOP!" I caught him, clasping my hand over his mouth before he finished the rhyme.

"Frankie! Leave your sister alone," Mrs. Baxter called out from the kitchen.

I looked him straight in the eye. "Francisco Álvarez,

if you breathe a word of this to anyone, I promise that I'll tell all your friends that you still sleep with a teddy bear by your pillow."

"I only do that because Mamá and Papá gave it to me. It's not like I'm a baby or something."

"So what? Do you want me to tell your friends or not?"

He looked down at the floor. "No."

"So, *nos entendemos*?"

Frankie rolled his eyes at me. "Yeah, we've got an understanding."

As he walked away, Frankie shook his head. "Man, Lucía, I liked it more when you were a pushover."

Chapter 34

CASTRO URGES MORE INTENSE COMMUNIST SPIRIT
FOR CUBANS; SAYS THE YOUNG WILL LIVE
UNDER COMMUNISM
—*MOBERLY MONITOR-INDEX*, MARCH 14, 1962

The frigid winter slowly began to give way to the extremely cold spring. The warming temperatures brought new life to Grand Island as everyone geared up for the large bird migration. Yearly festivals were held in honor of the migration, parties planned, even a parade was on the schedule. It was as if the whole town were celebrating the arrival of a long-lost friend.

Jennifer looked up at me as I stared off into space, lost in my thoughts. She leaned across the library table and whispered, "Pick anything. It really doesn't matter which."

I glanced down at the book in front of me. "It's just that Mrs. Brolin said she'd be displaying all our projects in the main library downtown. I want it to be really good. Plus, it's a big deal to everyone in town."

She rolled her eyes. "It's just a bird project. Really, it's not that important. Every year the teachers assign something to do with the big migration."

"Do you really get a lot of geese passing through here?" I flipped through the pages of *The Complete Pictorial Encyclopedia of the Midwest Migration*, looking for something special.

"More than you can shake a stick at."

"Huh?"

"It's a saying. It means *a lot*. Actually, something like fifteen million birds will fly through here. You'll see how people from all over come to see them. It's like a people migration, too."

"And you don't think that's cool?"

Jennifer shrugged. "I guess, but ugh, wait till you have to clean up after them. The birds, I mean, not the bird-watchers. They make a mess on the cars, the sidewalks, everything! It's disgusting! Betty even got pelted in the head last year walking into school."

The image of Betty wiping bird poop from her head was too funny. A loud giggle escaped into the quiet library.

Immediately the school librarian lowered her pointy glasses and shushed me.

Embarrassed, I sat up straight in the wooden chair and tried to look studious. Then I caught a glimpse of

Jennifer, who was acting like she was dodging bird pellets. Both of us started laughing.

The librarian pursed her lips and raised a single eyebrow. She normally saw me in the library by myself, scouring the newspapers for stories on what was happening in Cuba. She wasn't used to seeing me make noise. She cleared her throat and brought a finger to her lips.

For some strange reason, this made us laugh even more. To avoid being kicked out, we covered our faces with our notebooks. For a full minute, all you could see of us were notebooks bouncing up and down. Finally, we caught our breaths and tried to refocus on choosing my bird.

Jennifer glanced at her watch. "Look, it's almost four. Mom said she'd pick us up at about four-fifteen. We don't have much time left and I want to talk to you about what I should wear to the freshman spring dance. We're still going, right?"

I flipped through several more pages of the book. "I think Rita and Susan would kill us if we didn't go."

"Did you tell your parents?" Jennifer asked.

The mention of my parents made me pause and look up. "Uh-uh. Why risk them saying no? Besides, they already have a lot to worry about." I looked down at the page again. "I figure teachers will be chaperoning the dance and that should be good enough, right? I can always tell them later."

"That's true. Plus, missing our first high school dance would *definitely* not be cool." Jennifer put her hand over the book. "Do you think you'll dance with Eddie?"

I felt my entire body tighten up at the thought of dancing with Eddie. Until now, we'd just been friends, but that could all change so quickly. I hadn't really planned what to do if Eddie asked me to dance or if he tried to kiss me. I didn't want what happened with Manuel to repeat itself.

"Hey, I didn't mean to rattle your cage," Jennifer said. "He has no idea you even like him —"

"Kind of like him," I quickly corrected her.

"That's what I meant. We're all just going to have fun and hang out together. He may not even ask you to dance. Don't think of backing out on me, okay?"

I took a deep breath and muttered, "Okay." I tried to focus on the birds on the page again, but nothing seemed to interest me.

"Lucía, really, just pick anything. Here." She snapped the book shut and handed it to me. "Now just open it, and wherever it lands, that's it."

She was right. I didn't even know what I was looking for. I was making everything too complicated. It was just a school project. It didn't mean anything. There was nothing special about the bird I would choose.

I grabbed the book and closed my eyes. I popped it open to a random page in the middle, ready to accept of your countrymen, where even if it's tough, we're united in our suffering for a better Cuba.

It was all propaganda-speak.

You need to convince your parents to stay in Cuba or none of you will ever be allowed to return. You'll be people without a country, without a home, because the U.S. will never truly accept you. If you decide to stay where you are, then you are no better than all the other *gusanos* who've abandoned their homeland. Then you deserve to never see this place again. Tell me that you want to be part of the revolution, or else don't bother telling me anything at all.

The words stung.

Not because they were true, but because they were blatant lies. How could Ivette change so much? Erica had done nothing but help me and Frankie. Here I'd met some of the nicest and friendliest people in the world. People who cared for me.

My heart ached. I had wanted to go back to Cuba. To my parents. To my best friend. But that didn't seem possible anymore. That Cuba, that friend, simply didn't exist.

❊   ❊   ❊   ❊   ❊

whatever fate had in store. Then I saw something familiar.

A smile inched its way across my face.

There on the page was a white heron like the one I'd seen on the beach in Puerto Mijares. The book showed how some herons had migration routes that crossed through Cuba and Nebraska. This was it. This was my bird. A bird that lived in both my worlds.

❊   ❊   ❊   ❊   ❊

When I got to the Baxters', the table had already been set. The nice white tablecloth we used for Thanksgiving and Christmas was laid out. We were celebrating something.

"What's all this for?" I asked.

Mrs. Baxter was singing as she folded the napkins. "The doctor gave Mr. Baxter the all clear today. He'll be able to farm again." She twirled around the table as she fixed each place setting. "I swear, I haven't heard that man so happy in months. He's overjoyed, I tell you."

Mrs. Baxter's excitement was contagious. It felt like a party.

"Look what I made!" Frankie held a drawing of a man in the middle of a cornfield. On the top he'd written "Welcome Back!"

"He'll love it. You know, he keeps the picture you made him for Christmas in the drawer next to the bed. Mr. Baxter can be quite the sentimental guy."

I chuckled at the thought.

"No, really. He might not show it, but I know he feels it." Mrs. Baxter smiled. "He loves you kids."

A rumble in the driveway told us that Mr. Baxter had just pulled up.

"Oh good, he's here." Mrs. Baxter clasped her hands together. "I made all his favorites. Liver and onions, corn soufflé, green beans, dinner rolls. We're having a feast tonight!"

Mr. Baxter walked in and, without saying a word, took off his coat and hat, like always.

"I'm so happy!" Mrs. Baxter threw herself around him.

Mr. Baxter stood motionless for a second, then slowly put his arms around her waist. "Me too," he whispered.

Frankie squeezed in between them to show off his latest drawing.

"Hmm, looks quite a bit like me," Mr. Baxter said.

Frankie jumped up and down. "And see, the corn is high. Ready to be picked."

Mr. Baxter put a hand on Frankie's shoulder. "I see. You just might make a good farmer one day."

"Maybe . . . or an astronaut." Frankie stuck out his arms and pretended to fly around the room.

Mrs. Baxter stifled a laugh. "Oh, Frankie, you're too much!"

"Congratulations, Mr. Baxter. I'm very happy for you," I said.

"Thank you, Lucía." He went to his coat and pu something out of one pocket. "This came for you."

Mr. Baxter handed me an envelope with no r address.

"I'll read it later," I said, folding it into m pocket.

* * * * *

After dinner, Mr. Baxter decided to survey t with Frankie. Mrs. Baxter was on the phone friend Gladys, so I settled onto the lime green living room to read the evening paper. As I the envelope in my skirt pocket crinkled. I al want to read Ivette's letter. She really hadn' to most of my letters, and Mamá said Ivette the leader of the Jóvenes Rebeldes group i recruiting new kids for the brigades. It wa lieve that this was the same girl who'd g garten with me, who'd spent hours at my to music and planning my outfits, the o me the latest fashion magazines when the flu.

I opened the envelope. The letter w

Dear Lucía,

Have you completely sold y materialism of the American are falling into an obvious in kee trap. You should be her

It was dark as I walked in the bitter cold toward the mail-box. I'd just finished responding to Ivette's letter, telling her how wrong she was . . . about everything. That in the U.S., I'd found friends, happiness, and something she could never have with the revolution . . . freedom. It was here that people were free to choose their own path in life, free to speak their mind, free to have a different opinion, free to be themselves . . . all without fear.

I wrote about how she might be able to feel the Cuban soil under her feet or the smell the Caribbean Sea as it hit the powdery beaches, but I would carry Cuba with me wherever I went. That no matter what, I'd never stop loving my childhood home.

I glanced down at the envelope I was about to mail. A wave of sadness swept over me as I realized that my friendship with Ivette was ending. It had died a slow death over the past few months, and now it simply couldn't survive the different choices we were making. I knew that after reading my letter, Ivette would not write to me again.

I pulled open the mailbox, placed the envelope inside, and lifted the little red flag. I slowly turned around and trudged back through the snowy night into the warm and brightly lit Baxter house.

Chapter 35

CUBA READIES PROPAGANDA SPECTACLE—
1,183 PRISONERS GO ON TRIAL THURSDAY
—*SAN MATEO TIMES*, MARCH 24, 1962

The school gym was transformed. Instead of wooden bleachers and a huge scoreboard, all I saw was a world of large paper birds hanging from the rafters and five-foot cardboard flowers lining the walls. There were giant butterflies and ladybugs scattered among the blossoms. It was as if springtime had arrived in cartoonland. It was colorful, and a bit tacky, but I loved it.

"Lucía, over here!" Jennifer shouted above the music. She was talking with Doris and a few other girls who were on the decorations committee for the dance.

I walked toward them. Jennifer, with her slim yellow dress and blond hair, looked as bright as the sun itself. The other girls also looked like they were wearing their best spring dresses.

"Hi, everybody. The place looks great," I said.

"Ooh, I love your dress!" Doris exclaimed.

"It turned out gorgeous!" Jennifer agreed.

I looked down at the peach dress I was wearing. It was a simple sleeveless dress with a round collar and an A-line skirt. I had made it myself from a Simplicity pattern and cinched it at the waist with a white patent-leather belt borrowed from Mrs. Baxter.

I gave them all a mock little curtsy.

For a girl who'd had her first sewing lesson in home economics only six months earlier, it really was pretty nice.

"C'mon. Let's sit on the bleachers and see if we get asked to dance." Jennifer pulled me by the hand.

I resisted. "Instead, why don't we—"

"No excuses. Rita isn't coming 'cause she's sick, and Susan's already on the dance floor twisting away." She gave my arm a tug and I followed her to the stands.

As we walked over, I caught a glimpse of Eddie hanging out in the corner of the room with Nathan and a few others. They all looked nearly the same in their dark suits and thin ties, except Eddie towered over the other boys.

Jennifer and I sat on the first row of bleachers, next to a few other girls, and waited. I'd just gotten comfortable watching everyone else on the dance floor when Jennifer gave me a little nudge.

"Here they come," she whispered.

My heart sank as I saw Nathan and Eddie walking toward us. I kept remembering what had happened with Manuel. I didn't want a repeat of that night.

"Hi, girls," Eddie said.

"Hello, boys," Jennifer answered, twirling a strand of her hair.

Quiet.

It was an uncomfortable silence.

Eddie elbowed Nathan, who was standing in front of us shuffling his feet.

"Um . . . uh . . . yeah . . . so," Nathan stammered.

Eddie looked over at Jennifer. "So, Jenn, did you try to match the theme? Like Miss Sunshine or something?"

"What?" she asked.

"No, I mean Nathan and I were talking about how you both looked nice and stuff. You with your yellow dress and all."

"Like sunshine? Is that supposed to be funny, Eddie?" Jennifer crossed her arms.

"No, no. Hey, forget it. That just didn't come out right. Don't be mad. You want to dance?" He held out his hand. "I do a mean twist." He showed us his dance move and we all giggled.

And there it was.

Eddie had asked Jennifer to dance and not me.

Jennifer hesitated, but I nodded for her to go ahead.

"Okay," she said, standing up.

"Nathan, why don't you dance this song with Lucía and we can switch partners afterward. That okay, girls?" Eddie cautiously looked at the two of us.

"Sure," I answered.

Then I realized what had just happened and smiled.

Eddie was one clever boy.

❊   ❊   ❊   ❊   ❊

For the next hour, we danced to the latest rock 'n' roll songs. It was fun. When the song "Runaround Sue" came on, we all pointed to Sue Ellen Padgett, who tossed her hands in the air and spun around for us, as if on cue. The only ones who acted like they were completely bored were Betty and her group of followers. But eventually even they caved in and joined us on the dance floor. No one could resist the music and laughter. Eddie and I danced most of the songs together, and he kept making me laugh with all his silly moves. Everything was fine until "Blue Moon" started to play. It was a slow song.

I stood still on the dance floor as all the couples around me paired up to slow dance.

Eddie got closer.

All I could think was, Oh no, is everything going to get ruined?

He leaned in and whispered, "Want to go get something to drink and leave the slow dancing to the lovebirds?"

My shoulders dropped and I smiled. "Definitely," I said.

I crossed the dance floor without Eddie even trying to hold my hand. He only touched my back to make sure I didn't get bumped by a few dancing couples. I was feeling more and more relaxed being with him. He really was a good friend.

I watched him as he served us both something to drink. He had a bunch of freckles that covered his face, and his eyelashes seemed to fade toward the tips. He wasn't movie-star handsome, but there was definitely something attractive about him.

"What? Do I have something on my face?" he asked, handing me a cup.

"Oh no. I was just thinking about something." I'd been caught staring and I could feel my cheeks turning red.

"Are you having a good time?" he asked.

"Mmm-hmm." I looked over at Susan, who'd sat down on a nearby bleacher to catch her breath. She was fanning herself with a napkin.

"Seems like even Miss Dancing Queen had to take a break," Eddie said, pointing at Susan, who was now in the process of pulling her curly brown hair into a ponytail.

I looked up at Eddie. "Can I ask you a question?"

"Sure."

"You give everyone nicknames, why not me?"

Eddie shrugged. "Don't know. With you it's different." He looked down at his feet and stuffed his hands in his pockets. "It's hard to come up with just one word that really describes you."

My heart fluttered a little. He was so sweet, but I could see that he was uncomfortable. I needed to get us back to how we'd been just a few moments earlier. I gave him a light punch in the arm. It was the only thing I could think to do.

"What was that for?" He playfully rubbed his arm as if I'd really hurt him.

"Just for being Eddie." I smiled. "C'mon, let's take Susan a drink before she faints."

"Hmm, with a swing like that I might have a name for you after all . . . Champ."

I grinned, because tonight that was exactly how I felt.

Chapter 36

ONCE-PROSPEROUS CUBA SINKS UNDER SOCIALISM
—*WISCONSIN STATE JOURNAL*, MARCH 26, 1962

"You want to drive?" Mrs. Baxter dangled the keys in front of me.

She already knew the answer.

"Yes, ma'am!" I said.

"Oh, wait. Let's leave a note for Mr. Baxter." She took out a piece of paper and scribbled something on it. "You never know, he may come in from tilling the field a little early, and wonder where I went on a Monday."

Vacation on a school day . . . teacher workdays were the best.

I glanced at my watch. It was almost one o'clock, and although Frankie had already been picked up and taken to a friend's house, I still had to get to Grand Island before the matinee started. Jennifer had decided to celebrate her birthday with a movie, just like we'd done with mine, except this time several people were meeting us at the theater to see *West Side Story*... including Eddie and Nathan. Afterward we'd all go to the malt shop for cheeseburgers and milk shakes.

Mrs. Baxter followed me out to the porch, handing over the keys as she closed the door. "You know, I'm so happy Gladys started our weekly canasta games again. Ever since her daughter moved away, she's been in such a state. I can only imagine what they said about me when Carl moved away."

Just as I stepped off the porch, the phone inside rang.

"It's probably Jennifer wanting to know if I already left," I said.

The phone rang again.

Mrs. Baxter turned around and went back inside. "Just in case, I should answer it. Could be Frankie. Better safe than sorry," she said over her shoulder.

Mejor precaver que tener que lamentar. Same thing Mamá used to say. It was like a mother's unwritten motto.

I looked down at my hands. Mrs. Baxter and I had painted our nails berry pink a few days before, and for the first time, I didn't cry remembering the scene at the park. *I'm stronger now,* I thought.

"Oh yes . . . hold on." Mrs. Baxter motioned for me to come inside. "She's here. *Un momento.*"

Un momento? Why was she speaking in Spanish? We hadn't placed a call to Cuba.

Mrs. Baxter held out the phone. "Lucía, it's your mother."

I quickly grabbed it, my heart racing. Mamá had never phoned us. It was almost impossible to make that type of call from Cuba, especially now that Papá wasn't working.

"Mamá?" I held my breath.

"*Sí, Lucía. Soy yo. Mi hija,* I only have a minute, but your father and I need to tell you something."

"*¿Qué?*" It had to be bad for her to call. I felt like I should be sitting down.

"My exit visa was approved this morning. I was told I have seven days to leave the country or I have to stay indefinitely."

I wanted to do a little dance. My parents were coming. Finally, after almost a year, I'd get to see them again. "Mamá, that's great! Can you and Papá get plane tickets? Do you need money? I have some saved up."

"No, that's not it. I mean, yes, we will need some money, but it's just . . . it's just . . . ."

"What?" I asked.

"My visa got approved, but they won't approve your father's."

Everything around me stopped. The clock ticking in the hallway, the crackling on the phone line, the sound of the wind blowing through the open front door. I was in a soundless tunnel.

"Lucía? Lucía, are you still there?"

I slowly nodded.

I heard Mamá talking to someone else. "I think she hung up."

Papá came on the line. *"Lucía Margarita Álvarez, ¡habla!"* Papá's voice snapped me out of my daze.

"I'm here, I'm here."

"Oh, Lucy, listen, your mother doesn't want to go. I've already told her that I will not have her stay here. She needs to be with you and Frankie."

"But, Papá, what about you? You're not even well yet. Mamá says you can barely walk on that leg."

"I'll figure something out. Don't worry. I will get to my family. It may not be as quick as I like, but I'll get there. I love you, Lucy. Now talk to your mother."

Before I could respond, Mamá was back on the line. She was crying.

"Lucía, I don't know. If your father makes me go . . ." She sighed. "Well, I was thinking we'd live in Miami to be closer to Cuba and other exiles, but it seems like you have friends there in Nebraska."

I'd go anywhere to be with my parents, but I had already started a life in Grand Island. "Mamá, come here. We'll figure things out."

"But your father." Mamá's breathing was heavy. "You know they're doing this on purpose. First separating us from you and your brother, and now making me choose between my husband and my children. They want to destroy the family so that the only thing people have left is this stupid revolution. *¡Los odio! ¡A todos!* I hate them all!"

I tried to stay calm. She was right. They were doing this to make life difficult for those who didn't love the revolution above all else. "Mamá, fly to Nebraska. Trust Papá. He'll get to us. But you have to come. They may never let you out again."

"I know, I know." She sounded like a little girl.

"I'll take care of everything. You'll see."

"*Está bien*. I love you, Lucía. I'll see you in a few days."

My heart was breaking. I wanted both my parents to come over, but more than that, I knew how afraid Mamá must be at the thought of leaving Papá behind. "*Te quiero*, Mamá. Give Papá a kiss for me."

I slowly hung up the phone and looked up at Mrs. Baxter's expectant eyes.

"My mother is allowed to leave, but not my father."

"Oh, Lucía!" Mrs. Baxter opened her arms.

I didn't hesitate. I ran straight into them, and then we both cried.

Chapter 37

CUBA SLIPS AWAY FROM EXILES' DREAMS
—*THE CAPITAL*, APRIL 2, 1962

It had been a week since Mamá had called, and the Baxters and I had not stopped making plans. First, Mrs. Baxter persuaded her friend Gladys to let Mamá and us stay in the guest cottage behind her house. Mrs. Baxter explained that Gladys's daughter had used it as an art studio before moving to New York, but that now it sat empty. Plus, while visiting Gladys, she'd get to see us, too.

Then the parishioners at St. Mary's pitched in, donating items to furnish the cottage. We got everything from a frying pan to a small sofa. Mr. Baxter picked everything up, and before you knew it, we had the place looking pretty nice.

Mrs. Baxter even got her brother to hire Mamá to help count inventory on the weekends. It wasn't the life we used to have, but that life didn't exist in Cuba, either.

"I wish Papá could come, too," Frankie said, smoothing back his greased hair.

"I know, but it's really not up to him." I gazed at the large airport clock. Mamá's flight was due to arrive in about five minutes.

Five minutes. Three hundred seconds. Why did the clock's second hand have to move so slowly?

"She's going to be amazed at how much you've both grown. I simply can't wait to meet her. Lucía, do you think I look all right? I want to make a good impression." Mrs. Baxter adjusted her skirt.

"You look fine, Helen," Mr. Baxter answered for me. "The girl has other things on her mind."

I smiled. "She'll love you, but not because of anything you could wear."

She squeezed my arm. "I'm going to miss you so much, Lucía. I'll be visiting Gladys now more than ever."

"Poor Gladys," Mr. Baxter muttered as he adjusted his tie.

Frankie laughed and I jabbed him in the ribs.

"Look." Mrs. Baxter pointed to a sign over the airline counter. Flight 24 from Chicago had just arrived. Mamá was here!

I smoothed the wrinkles in my dress. We were all wearing our very best clothes, but I was worried about what Mamá would think when she saw us.

Frankie had grown about three inches, but he still looked more or less the same. I, on the other hand, was different.

Not only had my appearance changed with my new haircut, makeup, and growing curves, but I felt different inside. Somewhere between that plane ride out of Cuba and the drive to Lincoln to pick up Mamá, I had grown up.

Mamá's little girl wasn't here, but would she like the new me? Maybe I shouldn't have worn any makeup. But this was the new me. Yet if she saw me and didn't approve, then what?

I fidgeted with the buttons on my sweater.

What would she think of the Baxters, Jennifer . . . even Eddie?

The excited butterflies in my stomach turned on me. They were rising up to my throat. I felt like I was going to be sick.

What if Mamá thought I'd abandoned everything she'd taught me? What if I disappointed her?

Frankie pulled my arm. "Do you think Mamá will be upset that I love Mrs. Baxter?"

Before I could answer, Mrs. Baxter took Frankie's hand and inched forward. "Here we go," she said.

A stewardess opened two big doors, and a few people started to walk past us.

"Flight twenty-four?" Mr. Baxter asked a passenger who stopped to buy a newspaper.

The man nodded.

Frankie clung to Mrs. Baxter's waist as I tried to force my eyes to see farther through the crowd.

"Frankie! Lucía!" a voice called out.

It was Mamá.

She was weaving between and around people, trying to get to us. Frankie darted toward her. She looked the same as the last time I'd seen her. I even recognized the dress she was wearing. In a moment she had dropped her purse and lifted Frankie off the ground, smothering him with kisses.

Tears ran past my cheeks and down my neck. I felt as if I were moving in slow motion, every step bringing me only slightly closer to Mamá.

What would she say? What would she think of me?

Then I was in her arms. Mamá was crying and laughing at the same time. She kissed away my tears and looked at me. Really looked at me.

I waited.

She shook her head. "*Ay,* Lucía, you look so grown-up! *¡Qué bella estás!* You've become such a beautiful young lady!"

"Mamá," I cried, burying my head in her neck. "*Ay,* Mamá!"

"I am so proud of you," she whispered in my ear.

Several people had gathered around us, watching the emotional reunion.

Then from down the hallway, a flash of color caught my eye.

Bright red.

"Oh!" I gasped.

It was Papá, looking older and more frail. He was walking with Mamá's red umbrella as his cane.

"Lucy! Frankie!" he shouted, hobbling his way to us.

"Thank you, Lord!" Mrs. Baxter exclaimed.

We let go of Mamá to devour Papá with hugs and kisses.

"*¿Cómo?* How were you able to?" My brain was almost unable to accept that he was here.

"I told you I'd find a way." He smiled.

I breathed in the familiar smells of his cologne and cigars. "But they wouldn't give you a visa."

He dropped the umbrella and stroked my hair. "Details aren't important. I have friends in the underground who helped me. Plus, some of those Cuban officers have a price."

There was no need to know any more. I didn't care.

As we all hugged, I caught a glimpse of Mr. and Mrs. Baxter wiping away their own tears. They were happy for us. Even Mr. Baxter was smiling.

I bent down to pick up that beautiful red umbrella. Mamá was right. Red stood for strength. The strength of our family. We would start over in a new place and be just as strong as before.

I smiled as Papá shook Mr. Baxter's hand and Mamá gave Mrs. Baxter a hug.

The Álvarez family was together again. All of us. Here, in our new country.

I took a deep breath and slowly let it out.

It was good to be home.

Author's Note

The Red Umbrella is a fictional story based on very real events. From 1960 to 1962, the parents of over fourteen thousand Cuban children made the heart-wrenching decision to send their sons and daughters to the United States . . . alone. My parents and mother-in-law were among these children who were not only separated from their families but also separated from their country and culture.

Since this story is part of my family history, much of my research began at home. Asking my parents questions and remembering all the stories I'd heard growing up was the first step. As I dug deeper, I realized that this was not just a personal story, it was also an important part of American history. In fact, this was the largest exodus of unaccompanied children *ever* in the history of the Western Hemisphere, yet there wasn't much written about it, especially from the point of view of the children who experienced the upheaval. I wanted to change that.

In *The Red Umbrella,* as in real life, families were torn apart and friendships broken because of the Cuban revolution of 1959. Throughout the book, readers can catch a glimpse of what was happening in Cuba by looking at the newspaper headlines that begin each chapter. But the reasons behind this exodus of children were much more complex than the headlines suggest.

It all started with Fidel Castro's rise to power in 1959. At first, many people believed in Castro and his promise to make life better for all Cubans. However, as the months passed, it became apparent that Castro meant to retain complete control of the country by any means necessary. This included stripping away the right to private property, barring free speech, censoring the press, and limiting religious freedom. As people voiced their concern about what was happening, the response from Castro's Communist government was to label these people anti-revolutionary and to place them in jail or even execute them.

It was during this time that a rumor began to circulate that Cuban children's lives would be dictated by the government as well. The fact that some kids had already been sent to study in Russia added to the fear that soon *all* children would be removed from their parents' homes to be indoctrinated in government boarding schools or in the Soviet Union. The loss of freedoms, the fear of persecution, and the idea of losing their children to the Communist government forced many parents into making a previously unthinkable decision.

They would save their children by sending them to the United States.

And so, in 1960, a plan was hatched to help Cuban children escape the Communist island. The plan required the secret transport of documents, an underground network, and the courageous actions of people in the United States and Cuba. For the next two years, Cuban children arrived in Miami, Florida, by the planeload in what would eventually be called Operation Pedro Pan.

Many of these children had family or friends who picked them up once they arrived in Miami, but about half of the kids had no one. These temporarily orphaned children were placed by the Catholic Welfare Bureau with host families or in orphanages throughout the United States. It was there that these boys and girls waited to be reunited with their parents. Meanwhile, in Cuba, many parents were seeking exit visas to be able to leave their homeland and join their children in the United States. During this time, government institutions were being transformed by the Castro regime, and there was no standard as to whose visa would be granted. Approval was left to the whim of government officials, and so some parents resorted to using bribes and political influence to secure their freedom. Eventually, most parents were able to join their children in the United States after being separated for a period ranging from a few months to several years. However, a few weren't as lucky and never saw their children again.

As for my parents and mother-in-law, they were fortunate enough to be reunited with their families. They were able to live the American dream and, just like Lucía in the story, discovered that home is not a physical place but can be found wherever you have people who love and accept you.

Acknowledgments

First, I'd like to thank God for giving me a life so full of blessings, joy, and just enough difficulty to appreciate it all. I am truly grateful.

Next, I'd like to give a special thank-you to my grandparents, who made the heartbreaking decision to send their children, alone, to the United States. Because of their foresight, our family has become part of the American dream. *¡Gracias, Abo, Abi,* and *Abicheli!*

In almost the same breath, I would like to thank my parents, who raised me with an appreciation for my Cuban heritage and a love for the USA. Your courage and strength as teenagers and your unyielding desire to make a better life in your adopted country are a constant source of pride for me. Thank you for your unwavering support and unconditional love. You are my heroes.

I also want to thank my sister, who has always been my sounding board and best friend. I know I can always count on you.

Thank you to my husband, who believes everything I write is perfect . . . even when it's not. You fill my life with love and happiness. I am forever grateful that you encouraged me to follow my dreams.

Thank you to my sons, who inspired me to pursue my passion for writing. You are my greatest joy and I am very lucky to be your mother. I hope this book reminds you of your family's past as you follow your own destiny.

Thank you to my mother-in-law, who shared her own experiences as a Pedro Pan child and whom I'm lucky enough to have in my life.

For the world's best brother-in-law, who "volunteered" to do my book trailer. You rock!

To all my aunts, uncles, cousins, nieces, and nephews . . . thank you for adding so much to my life. Comparisons to the movie *My Big Fat Greek Wedding* do not do justice to the amazing, supportive, loud, and crazy family that we are.

There are also several people in the writing world whom I am fortunate enough to consider friends and who helped make this book a reality.

Beginning with my amazing editor, Nancy Siscoe, who saw the potential of this book within the first ten pages and encouraged me to finish it ASAP. Thank you for all your guidance and advice. You are the best!

Thank you to author and task-keeper Danielle Joseph, who pushed me to finish this book by checking on my progress with her nightly e-mails.

Special thanks to all my SCBWI friends and especially my critique group partners: Adrienne Sylver, Linda Bernfeld, Gaby Triana, Liz Trotta, Mary Thorp, Marta Magellan, Tere Starr, Ruth Vander Zee, Marjetta Geerling, Michelle Delisle, Kerry Cerra, Mindy Alyse Weiss, Mindy Dolandis, and my mentor, Joyce Sweeney. The advice and feedback I receive from all of you has shaped my writing, and I know that I am a better writer because of it.

To the star of my book trailer, Stephanie Freire, and the supporting cast members, Gaby Reyes, Madeleine Saade, Emily Ferradaz, Adriana Perez-Siam, Lauren Medina, Aliana Zamorano, Michael Schnabel, Derek Diaz, Frank

Sancho, Martha Alcazar, Priscilla Valls, and Alison Wood Griñan . . . thank you all for adding a new dimension to the book!

A big thank-you also goes to everyone who shared their knowledge of Cuba and Operation Pedro Pan with me, especially Jorge "Jay" Guarch, Jr., Lynn Guarch-Pardo, Frank Angones, and Dr. Brian Latell.

Finally, to everyone at the Knopf/Random House family who worked on all the different phases of this book . . . thank you so much for helping make *The Red Umbrella* possible.

Spanish words and phrases used in *The Red Umbrella*

a mí no me gusta eso (ah mee noh meh GOO-stah EH-soh): I don't like that

abuela (ah-BWEH-lah): grandmother

adiós (ah-dee-OHS): good-bye

anís (ah-NEES): star anise—used in herbal teas

apúrate (ah-POO-rah-teh): hurry up

aquí (ah-KEE): here

arroz con pollo (ah-ROHS kohn POH-yoh): traditional Spanish dish of rice and chicken

baja (BAH-hah): to fall

basta (BAH-stah): enough

besos (BEH-sohs): kisses

bien (bee-EN): fine, well

bobo (BOH-boh): stupid, used informally

bolsillo (bohl-SEE-yoh): pocket

brigadista (bree-gah-DEE-stah): member of the brigades

bueno (BWEH-noh): good

buenos días (BWEH-nohs DEE-ahs): good morning

café con leche (kah-FAY kohn LEH-cheh): coffee with milk

cao (kow): crow

cepillos de dientes (seh-PEE-yohs deh dee-EN-tes): toothbrushes

charco de fango (CHAHR-koh deh FAHN-goh): puddle of mud

chica (CHEE-kah): girl

chisme (CHEEZ-meh): gossip

cinco (SEEN-koh): five

claves (KLAH-vehs): a percussion instrument made up of a pair of short, cylindrical rods

cobardes (koh-BAHR-des): cowards

comas (KOH-mahs): eat

cómo (KOH-moh): how

cómo estás (KOH-moh es-TAHS): how are you?

cómo te extraño (KOH-moh teh eks-TRAH-nyo): how I miss you

compañeros (kohm-pah-NYAY-rohs): companions

comprendes (kohm-PREN-des): understand

comunista (koh-moo-NEES-tah): Communist

crema de afeitar (KREH-mah deh ah-fay-TAHR): shaving cream

croqueta (kroh-KEH-tah): croquette—a small fried food roll

cuanto (KWAHN-toh): how much, how many, how long

cuatro (KWAH-troh): four

cuídate (KWEE-dah-teh): take care

dime la verdad (DEE-meh lah vehr-DAHD): tell me the truth

Dios mío (dee-OHS MEE-oh): my God

ducha (DOO-chah): shower

es (es): it is

escucha (es-KOO-chah): listen

escuelas privadas (es-KWEH-lahs pree-VAH-dahs): private schools

está bien (es-TAH bee-EN): okay

estoy (es-TOY): I am

feliz año nuevo (feh-LEES AH-nyoh noo-EH-voh): happy New Year

feliz cumpleaños (feh-LEES koom-pleh-AH-nyohs): happy birthday

Feliz Navidad (feh-LEES nah-vee-DAHD): Merry Christmas

flan (flahn): creamy custard-like dessert

frío (FREE-oh): cold

gabinete (gah-bee-NEH-tay): medicine cabinet

gracias (GRAH-see-ahs): thank you

gusanos (goo-SAH-nohs): worms

habla (AH-blah): speak, talk

hasta mañana (AH-stah mah-NYAH-nah): until tomorrow (good night)

hermano (ehr-MAH-noh): brother

hijos / hija / hijo (EE-hohs/ EE-hah / EE-hoh): children / daughter / son

hola (OH-lah): hello

hombre (OHM-breh): man

hoy (oy): today

imperialista (eem-peh-ree-ah-LEES-tah): imperialist

increíble (een-kreh-EE-bleh): incredible

invierno (een-vee-EHR-noh): winter

Jóvenes Rebeldes (HOH-veh-nes reh-BEL-des): Rebel Youth—the Communist youth movement in Cuba

las cosas cambian (lahs KOH-sahs KAHM-bee-ahn): things change

lechón (LAY-chohn): roasted pig

levántate (leh-VAHN-tah-teh): get up

lindo / bien lindo (bee-EN LEEN-doh): pretty/ very pretty

los odio a todos (lohs OH-dee-oh a TOH-dohs): I hate them all

Los Pioneros (lohs pee-oh-NEH-rohs): The Pioneers— Communist youth movement for small children

los queremos también (lohs keh-REH-mohs tahm-bee-EN): we love you, too

maíz (mah-EEZ): corn

más (mahs): more

mejor precaver que tener que lamentar (meh-HOR preh-kah-VEHR keh ten-EHR keh lah-men-TAHR): better safe than sorry

mentira (men-TEE-rah): a lie

minutos (mee-NOO-tohs): minutes

momento (moh-MEN-toh): moment

mujer (moo-HEHR): woman

nacionalización (nah-see-oh-nah-lee-sah-see-OHN): nationalization

nada (NAH-dah): nothing

nido de parasitos (NEE-doh deh pah-rah-SEE-tohs): nest of parasites

nieve (nee-EH-veh): snow

niños (NEE-nyohs): children

no fue nada (noh fweh NAH-dah): it was nothing

no importa (noh eem-POR-tah): it doesn't matter

no sé (no seh): don't know

Nochebuena (noh-cheh-BWEH-nah): Christmas Eve

nos entendemos (nohs en-ten-DEH-mohs): we understand each other

nosotros (noh-SOH-trohs): us

noventa (noh-VEN-tah): ninety

oye (OH-yeh): listen

palomilla (pah-loh-MEE-yah): a very thin steak

pan cubano (pahn koo-BAH-noh): Cuban bread

para (PAH-rah): for

paredón (pah-reh-DOHN): wall used by the firing squad for executions

pecera (peh-SEH-rah): fishbowl

perdóname (pehr-DOHN-ah-meh): excuse me

perfecto (pehr-FEK-toh): perfect

permiso (pehr-MEE-soh): permission, permit

pero (PEH-roh): but

picadillo (pee-kah-DEE-yoh): ground beef hash

plato de segunda mesa (PLAH-toh deh seh-GOON-dah MEH-sah): literally, second table's plates—leftovers

por favor (por fah-VOR): please

por qué (por keh): why?

pórtate bien (POR-tah-teh bee-EN): behave well

preciosa (preh-see-OH-sah): precious

presta atención (PRES-tah ah-ten-see-OHN): pay attention

puedes ir a jugar (PWEH-des eer ah HOO-gahr): you can go play

qué (keh): what?

qué bella estás (keh BEH-yah es-TAS): how beautiful you are

qué maldito (keh mahl-DEE-toh): what a devil

qué dijiste (keh dee-HEE-steh): what did you say?

qué falta de respeto (keh FAHL-tah deh res-PEH-toh): what disrespect

qué habrá pasado (keh ah-BRAH pah-SAH-doh): wonder what happened

qué haces (keh AH-ses): what are you doing?

qué hemos hecho (keh EH-mohs EH-choh): what have we done?

qué pasa (keh PAH-sah): what's wrong?

qué pasó (keh pah-SOH): what happened?

qué se cree él (keh seh kreh el): what does he think?

qué te vas a poner (keh teh vahs ah poh-NEHR): what are you going to wear?

quién es (kee-EN es): who is it?

quinceañera (keen-seh-NYEHR-ah) / *quinces* (KEEN-sehs): fifteenth birthday party—similar to a sweet sixteen party

repítelo (reh-PEE-teh-loh): repeat it

revolución (reh-voh-loo-see-OHN): revolution

sí (see): yes

siéntate (see-EN-tah-teh): sit down

sigue (SEE-geh): continue

sobrina (soh-BREE-nah): niece

socialismo o muerte (soh-see-ah-LEES-moh oh moo-EHR-teh): socialism or death

soy yo (soy yo): it's me

tarea (tah-REH-ah): homework

te quiero (teh kee-EHR-oh): I love you

te voy a extrañar (teh voy ah eks-trah-NYAHR): I'm going to miss you

tilo (TEE-loh): linden flowers—used in herbal teas

tío (TEE-oh): uncle

todo bien (TOH-doh bee-EN): everything's okay

tranquila (trahn-KEE-lah): relax

tres reyes magos (tres REH-yes MAH-gohs): the three wise men from the Bible

tú eres (too EH-res): you are

usted conoce (oo-STED koh-NOH-seh): do you know?

vámonos (VAH-moh-nohs): let's go

ven acá (ven ah-KAH): come here

vida (VEE-dah): life

viva la revolución (VEE-vah lah reh-voh-loo-see-OHN): long live the revolution

y tú (ee too): and you

yo se leer (yo seh leh-EHR): I know how to read

yo soy (yo soy): I am